The Guar
the Phoenix Stone

Mastan Momin

CONTENTS

AWAKENING

Aidan's tale begins in the peaceful embrace of Ehime, a hidden treasure nestled deep within the lush Faelorian Forest. This haven of pure beauty and timeless wonder cradled Aidan throughout his early years. As the firstborn child of parents who were deeply involved in the village's life, Aidan's father, Vilem, was a master blacksmith who crafted exceptional weapons and tools that resonated with the wisdom of the time. Aidan's mother, Elara, was a renowned healer with a vast knowledge of herbs and remedies, which attracted people from neighbouring villages seeking her aid. From the moment Aidan took his first breath, it was clear he was a child of nature with a boundless curiosity extending beyond the village's borders. His emerald eyes, reflecting the lush hues of the surrounding forest, held a glimmer of wonder, hinting at an inherent magic that set him apart from his peers. His connection with the natural world deepened as he grew, and the ancient trees whispered secrets he could only hear. Ehime itself seemed to recognise him as one of its own.

The sprawling expanse of the Faelorian Forest served as a haven for Aidan, offering him a wellspring of inspiration and a sense of peace. As he roamed among the towering trees and hidden groves, he was entranced by the melodies of unknown creatures and moved by the natural rhythms surrounding him. Each day brought new marvels to uncover, from the shimmering wings of delicate butterflies to the sparkling dewdrops that adorned spiderwebs at dawn. The forest became Aidan's mentor, and the wild beasts his comrades. His bond with nature deepened as he matured, and his

3

mother, Elara, quickly recognised his growing affinity for the forest and its mysteries. She encouraged his connection, sharing the ancient wisdom of herbalism and healing passed down for generations. Guided by her gentle hand, Aidan learned to differentiate between the countless plants that carpeted the forest floor, gaining insight into their medicinal properties and crucial role in maintaining the delicate balance of life.

In contrast, his father, Vilem, introduced him to the forge, where roaring flames transformed raw metal into weapons and tools. Under his father's watchful eye, Aidan learned the art of blacksmithing. He laboured tirelessly, honing his skills and crafting intricate works of iron and steel, imbuing each piece with a piece of his soul. The village, too, benefited from Aidan's dedication to his craft, as his father's forge became renowned for producing weapons of unmatched quality. Life in Ehime was idyllic, a harmonious blend of nature and craftsmanship. Still, it was destined to change in a way no one could have foreseen.

On the evening before Aidan's sixteenth birthday, the tranquil community of Ehime was suddenly and violently attacked by a horde of malevolent creatures known as the Maelthorn. These vicious beings had one objective: to take possession of the Phoenix Stone, a precious and highly sought-after gem the villagers had protected for generations. Aidan's family sprang into action without hesitation, each member utilising their unique skills and strengths to defend their home. His father, a master weapon-smith, wielded his finely crafted blades with deadly precision. At the same time, his mother Elara, an expert in herbs, tended to the wounded with remarkable skill and care.

Despite being untrained in combat, Aidan fearlessly joined the fray, fighting alongside his fellow villagers with all the courage he could muster. The battle was intense and gruelling, but the villagers refused to give up. And then, in pure astonishment, Aidan's hands suddenly burst into flames. With this newfound power, he unleashed a torrent of otherworldly energy that utterly decimated the Maelthorn and saved the village from certain destruction. It was a remarkable display of bravery and strength lying dormant within him, waiting for the perfect moment to emerge. A hushed awe swept through the villagers as they beheld the incredible spectacle. Ehime's inhabitants and their fear giving way to gratitude hailed Aidan as a hero. Yet, Aidan stood amidst the battle's remnants, a bewildered young man grappling with the enormity of what he had just unleashed. How had he conjured fire from within himself? What did it mean for his future?

In the following days, Aidan sought answers from his parents, the keepers of wisdom in his life. His mother, Elara, recognised that Aidan's newfound abilities were inexorably tied to the enigmatic Phoenix Stone of Ehime. She spoke of ancient legends, of a chosen one destined to be the guardian of the Phoenix Stone, a protector imbued with the power of fire, a Nura'el. The Phoenix Stone, a mystical artefact of profound significance, had been entrusted to the village by the forest itself. It was rumoured to house the essence of the Faelorian Forest, a source of life and magic that sustained the entire region. Elara explained that Aidan's abilities manifested the deep connection between him and the Phoenix Stone. This bond bound them together inextricably. But this newfound role as a Nura'el carried a weighty burden. The Maelthorn, sensing the awakening of the Phoenix Stone's power, would not rest until they had wrested it from Ehime's grasp. The village was no longer safe, and Aidan, with a heavy heart, made the painful decision to depart. He embarked on a solitary journey, leaving behind his home and loved ones to unlock the full extent of his powers and protect the Phoenix Stone from the clutches of the Maelthorn. With his parents' blessings, Aidan departed with a satchel filled with herbs, remedies, and a heartfelt letter from his mother, offering guidance and solace in the face of the unknown.

Aidan's connection to nature grew stronger as he ventured deeper into the Faelorian Forest. He encountered mystical creatures, sentient beings that recognised him as the chosen Nura'el. They shared their ancient wisdom, teaching him the secrets of the forest and the Phoenix Stone's magic. The forest, he discovered, was not merely a backdrop to his journey but an active participant, guiding him toward his destiny. Aidan refined his abilities during his travels, learning to wield the flames within him as a skilled artisan would craft a masterpiece. As the days turned weeks and weeks into months, Aidan's reputation as a Nura'el spread far and wide. Word of his courageous deeds spread to far-off communities, and individuals turned to him for aid in their most desperate moments. He became a beacon of hope in a world threatened by the looming darkness of the Maelthorn. Yet, despite his growing prowess, Aidan was haunted by doubts and unanswered questions. What was the true nature of the Phoenix Stone's power? Why had he been chosen as its guardian? And what role did the Maelthorn play in the grand tapestry of destiny?

One fateful evening, as Aidan camped beneath the starlit canopy of the Faelorian Forest, he received a vivid dream – a vision bestowed upon him by the Phoenix Stone itself. In this ethereal vision, he witnessed the Phoenix Stone's creation, forged by ancient druids in communion with the forest's essence. He observed the rise of the Maelthorn, creatures born of a twisted perversion of magic, whose insidious intent was to corrupt the Phoenix Stone's power for their nefarious purposes. In the dream, Aidan stood as the forest's chosen protector, the Nura'el. He beheld himself wielding the Phoenix Stone's power not as a destructive force but as an instrument of creation and renewal. The revelation was staggering, a destiny that seemed both monumental and inescapable. Yet, it brought a clarity of purpose that Aidan had long sought. Determined to confront the looming threat of the Maelthorn and unlock the Phoenix Stone's true potential, Aidan embarked on a quest to gather knowledge and allies. One such ally was Lyria, a skilled archer whose connection to the forest's creatures rivalled Aidan's. Her presence brought equilibrium to Aidan's fiery powers, and their friendship flourished into a deep bond of trust and camaraderie. Together, they confronted countless challenges, thwarted the Maelthorn's treacherous schemes, and uncovered forgotten truths about the Phoenix Stone and the Faelorian Forest.

As Aidan continued to confront different challenges, he delved deeper into the Phoenix Stone's magic. He learned to harness its power. He realised that the Phoenix Stone's essence encompassed fire, life, and renewal – a phoenix perpetually reborn from its own ashes. With this profound insight, Aidan and Lyria dared to confront the Maelthorn at one of their stronghold called Getsnake, a place contaminated by their twisted sorcery. It was a harrowing battle, a cataclysmic clash of elemental forces. Aidan drew upon the Phoenix Stone's most bottomless reservoirs of power. He wielded it not to obliterate but to purify, restore, and undo the malignancies wrought by the Maelthorn's corruption. The battle's climax loomed as Aidan faced the leader of Getsnake, a formidable adversary steeped in dark magic serving Maelthorn. He channelled the Phoenix Stone's essence in a cataclysmic crescendo of fire and determination, enveloping the malevolent creature in a blinding conflagration. In that ephemeral moment, Aidan became a living phoenix, a symbol of rebirth and renewal, as the Phoenix Stone's power cleansed the corruption from the Maelthorn's very soul.

The victory was hard-won, and the forest resounded with the jubilant cries of its defenders. The Maelthorn's menace had been vanquished from the Getsnake, and the Phoenix Stone was again secure. Aidan stood as a vigilant guardian of the Faelorian Forest, a protector of its ancient magic, and a symbol of hope for all who sought shelter beneath its emerald boughs. Yet, Aidan's journey was far from its conclusion. He recognised that his role as a Nura'el extended beyond the confines of defending the Phoenix Stone. It encompassed safeguarding the delicate equilibrium between nature and civilisation, using his abilities to protect and nurture the world around him.

THE CALL

The dense foliage of the Faelorian Forest loomed like a colossal green cathedral, its towering trees forming a tapestry of shadow and light beneath the dappled canopy. Sunlight filtered through emerald leaves, casting a soothing glow upon the forest floor. Aidan ventured deeper into the forest's heart. His powers had grown more robust, and his connection to the Phoenix Stone was now a constant presence, a reassuring hum in the background of his consciousness. His memory of his epic battle against the Maelthorn at Getsnake still burned brightly. Still, it was joined by a sense of purpose and clarity from the revelations of the Phoenix Stone's true power. As he explored the forest, he was drawn to a secluded glen bathed in soft golden light. There, beneath the canopy of ancient oaks, he felt a peculiar resonance, a beckoning that stirred his heart.

As he approached the glen, Aidan noticed an intricately carved stone altar at its centre, upon which a smattering of fragrant wildflowers rested. It was as though the forest itself had set the stage for a meeting of great importance. The air crackled with an almost tangible anticipation. Suddenly, a gentle breeze rustled through the leaves, and the forest sighed with ancient wisdom. A voice, soft as the murmur of a brook, whispered in Aidan's mind, "The time has come, Nura'el. Seek the one who will illuminate your path." Aidan's heart quickened. It was a message from the Phoenix Stone, indicating that his journey has begun. The forest was guiding him, and he deeply trusted its guidance. With each step, the glen seemed to come alive, its energy intensifying as Aidan approached

8

the altar. At that moment, the air around him shimmered with warm, iridescent light, and a figure began to materialise beside the stone altar. Aidan could hardly believe his eyes.

Before him stood a woman of ethereal beauty, her presence radiating a serenity that seemed to envelop the glen in an aura of tranquillity. Her long, flowing hair cascaded like liquid silver, and her eyes held the wisdom of countless ages. She was dressed in a robe adorned with intricate patterns reminiscent of leaves and flames, and a staff crowned with a crystal seemed to pulse with a soft, inner light. Aidan's breath caught in his throat as he realised he was in someone extraordinary's presence. A sense of reverence washed over him, and he sank to his knees, respectfully bowing. The woman extended her hand, her voice a gentle caress. "Rise, young Nura'el. You need not kneel before me." Aidan complied, standing before this enigmatic figure with awe and curiosity. "Who are you?" he asked, his voice trembling slightly. She smiled, her eyes filled with a knowing warmth. "I am Ophelia, guardian of the ancient prophecies and keeper of the forest's deepest secrets." Aidan felt a torrent of questions welling inside him as the weight of her words settled upon him. "Why have you appeared before me, Ophelia? What is my destiny, and how can I fulfil it?" Ophelia's gaze remained steady, her expression one of serene contemplation. "Your destiny, young one, is entwined with the Phoenix Stone and the ancient prophecy that foretells the renewal of the Faelorian Forest. You are the Nura'el, a guardian the forest chose to protect its magic and restore its balance. But there is much you have yet to learn."

Aidan's heart swelled with both anticipation and trepidation. He had longed for answers, for guidance, and now, in the presence of Ophelia, it seemed that the mysteries of his existence might finally be unveiled. "Your powers," Ophelia continued, "are a fraction of what they can become. The Phoenix Stone's essence is not limited to fire alone; it embodies nature's eternal cycle of creation and renewal. To unlock its full potential, you must embark on a journey of discovery, both within and beyond the boundaries of this forest." The gravity of her words sank in, and Aidan nodded solemnly. "I am ready to learn, Ophelia. I am ready to embrace my

9

destiny." Ophelia's smile deepened, and she gestured to the stone altar beside her. "Then, let us begin. Close your eyes, Aidan, and let the forest speak to you. Listen to its wisdom, for it has been your silent companion since the day you were born." Aidan did as she instructed, shutting his eyes and allowing the forest sounds to envelop him. He heard the rustling of leaves, the distant call of a hidden bird, and the gentle flow of a nearby stream. As he listened, the forest's symphony seemed to harmonise and coalesce into a melodic resonance that pulsed within him. Aidan felt more attuned to the forest's rhythms with each passing moment. It was as though he could sense the ebb and flow of life itself, the cyclical dance of birth, growth, and renewal. The Phoenix Stone's presence within him throbbed in time with the forest's song. Ophelia's voice, like a soft breeze, whispered in his mind. "You are now connected to the heart of the forest, Aidan. Feel its energy coursing through you, for you are an integral part of this tapestry of life." Aidan remained in this state of profound communion with the forest for what seemed like an eternity. It was as though he had transcended the boundaries of his physical form, becoming one with the ancient, primordial essence of the Faelorian Forest.

When he finally opened his eyes, he saw Ophelia gazing at him with approval. "You have taken your first step on this path, Aidan. But there is much more to learn, and your journey will lead you to wondrous and perilous places." He nodded, a newfound determination burning in his eyes. "Ophelia, rest assured that I am ready to embark on this journey, no matter the obstacles. I am committed to following this path until the end."

Under Ophelia's guidance, Aidan's training as a Nura'el began earnestly. Each day, they delved deeper into the forest, exploring its hidden glades, ancient groves, and secluded sanctuaries. Ophelia taught him to read the subtle signs of nature, discern the secrets whispered by the wind, and communicate with the forest's myriad creatures. Ophelia instructed Aidan in harnessing the Phoenix Stone's power in a secluded clearing adorned with vibrant wildflowers. She guided him in invoking fire, not as a destructive force, but as a tool of transformation and renewal. Aidan learned to shape flames with precision, heal wounds, and mend the forest's wounds with gentle fire caresses. Their training extended beyond the realm of fire manipulation. Ophelia revealed to Aidan the ancient rituals that bound him to the forest's magic. They performed ceremonies beneath the moonlit sky, invoking the blessings of the forest's spirits and strengthening Aidan's connection to the Phoenix Stone.

In these moments, Aidan could feel the forest responding to his presence as though it recognised him as its chosen guardian. Leaves rustled in approval, and the songs of birds took on a sweeter, more melodious tone. The forest was teaching him, guiding him, and he felt humbled by its wisdom.

Ophelia taught Aidan to commune with the ancient tree spirits, beings of immense wisdom who had witnessed the passing of centuries. They shared tales of the forest's history, battles against forces of darkness and nature's resilience. One particular tree spirit, an ancient oak named Hubert, became Aidan's mentor in understanding the intricate balance between life and decay. Hubert's gnarled branches reached high into the sky, and his voice was like the whisper of leaves in the wind. Under his guidance, Aidan discovered the delicate interplay between birth and death, between the fallen leaves that nourished the soil and the new growth that emerged from the forest floor. Hubert's wisdom extended to the Phoenix Stone itself. He revealed that the Phoenix Stone was a vessel of life's essence, a repository of nature's ceaseless cycle. Hubert reminded Aidan that his role as a Nura'el was not just about defending the Phoenix Stone but also about ensuring its power was used for the benefit of the land and its inhabitants.

Aidan and Ophelia were sitting beneath the sprawling branches of Hubert. Aidan finally voiced a question that had been weighing on his mind. "Ophelia, what of the Maelthorn? What role do they play in this grand tapestry of destiny?" Ophelia's gaze turned sombre, and she spoke with a hint of sadness. "The Maelthorn are a dark force, a perversion of magic that seeks to corrupt the Phoenix Stone and bend its power to their malevolent will. They are creatures born of greed, hatred, and a thirst for dominion over the natural world." Aidan's jaw tightened with determination. "I will not allow them to succeed. I will protect the Phoenix Stone with all my strength and knowledge." Ophelia nodded in approval. "Your resolve is commendable, Aidan, but you must remember that defeating the Maelthorn is not just a matter of force. It is a battle of light against darkness, and you must wield the Phoenix Stone's power with wisdom and compassion."

As weeks turned into months, Ophelia introduced Aidan to other aspects of his role as a Nura'el. With each passing day, Aidan's bond with Ophelia deepened, and she became not only his mentor but also a source of solace and guidance. They shared stories by the flickering light of campfires, their conversations ranging from the forest's mysteries to the intricacies of life's interconnectedness. The days became a seamless blend of training, exploration, and reflection. Aidan's powers continued growing, and he honed his ability to precisely manipulate fire. He learned to channel the Phoenix Stone's energy for healing and rejuvenating the forest's flora and fauna.

One morning, Ophelia led Aidan to a sacred grove hidden deep within the forest, where time seemed to stand still. At its centre stood an ancient oak, its massive trunk etched with centuries of history. This tree, known as the Primus, was a repository of the forest's memories and the guardian of an ancient tome, the Codex. The Codex was a volume of unparalleled knowledge, a compendium of the forest's secrets, flora and fauna, hidden realms, and the ancient prophecies that bound its fate to the Nura'el. Aidan's heart quickened as he beheld the Codex, its pages adorned with intricate illustrations and script that seemed to pulse with their own life. Ophelia guided him in deciphering the Codex's cryptic passages, revealing the forest's intricate web of life and magic. They read of the ancient druids who had crafted the Phoenix Stone and the rituals that could amplify its power. They uncovered prophecies about Aidan's role as a guardian, his trials and tribulations, and his ultimate destiny. As Aidan delved deeper into the Codex's pages, he became aware of a recurring symbol that appeared throughout the text – a blazing phoenix with wings outstretched, surrounded by a circle of leaves and flames. It symbolised renewal and rebirth, representing the eternal cycle of life and death that permeated the forest.

Ophelia placed a hand on his shoulder, her voice a gentle reassurance. "The phoenix is not just a symbol, Aidan; it reflects your destiny. You are the Nura'el, chosen by the forest to protect its magic and ensure its eternal renewal. Your path will be marked by trials, but remember that the phoenix rises from its ashes, stronger and more radiant than before." Aidan closed the Codex and turned to Ophelia. "I am ready, Ophelia. Ready to face whatever trials lie ahead and fulfil my destiny."

Under Ophelia's tutelage, Aidan's journey as a Nura'el continued, leading him deeper into the heart of the Faelorian Forest. The forest became his classroom, sanctuary, and source of inspiration as he honed his abilities and unravelled the mysteries of the Phoenix Stone. Their exploration often led them to hidden glades, where Aidan learned to commune with the forest's creatures. Ophelia taught him the language of birds, the songs of insects, and the silent conversations of the forest's inhabitants. With each encounter, Aidan's connection to the natural world deepened, and he understood that the forest itself was a living entity, a vast web of interconnected life. One day, as they ventured into a remote corner of the forest, Aidan encountered a wounded deer, its eyes filled with fear and pain. He touched the creature without hesitation, channelling the Phoenix Stone's energy to mend its injuries. The deer's wounds closed before his eyes, and it regarded him with a sense of gratitude that transcended language. Ophelia smiled, her eyes filled with pride. "You see, Aidan, your powers extend beyond fire. You have the gift of healing, of nurturing life. It is a reflection of the forest's resilience and its capacity for renewal."

Aidan's understanding of the forest's delicate balance deepened as they continued their journey. He witnessed the interdependence of its flora and fauna, how the growth of one species nourished another, and how life and death were inseparable facets of the same cycle. The forest was a tapestry of harmony, a testament to the enduring power of nature. Their quest also led them to encounter mystical creatures that inhabited the forest's hidden realms. Aidan met the luminous sprites that danced among the fireflies at dusk, the wise old dryads who guarded the ancient trees, and the elusive water spirits that sang enchanting melodies in the moonlit streams. Each encounter was a lesson in humility and wonder, a reminder of the vastness of the forest's magic. Throughout their journey, Ophelia continued to mentor Aidan in the art of fire manipulation. He learned to summon flames not with force but with the gentlest of intentions. He could shape fire into intricate patterns, illuminating the darkness with a dance of light and shadow. It was a reflection of his growing mastery over the Phoenix Stone's power.

Their journey also led them to encounters with ancient druids. The same mystical beings had crafted the Phoenix Stone ages ago. These enigmatic figures lived in harmony with the forest, their knowledge of its secrets passed down through generations. Under their guidance, Aidan delved into the rituals that could amplify the Phoenix Stone's power. One such ritual involved a ceremony beneath the full moon's light, where Aidan and Ophelia stood before a circle of ancient stones, each inscribed with symbols of nature's elements. Aidan channelled the Phoenix Stone's energy as the moon's silvery glow bathed them in its radiance, summoning flames that danced like ethereal fireflies around him. The druids chanted ancient incantations, their voices blending with the rustling leaves and the murmurs of the forest. In that moment, Aidan felt a profound connection to the Phoenix Stone, as though it resonated with the very heartbeat of the woods. The ritual amplified his powers, and he knew he had taken another step toward fulfilling his destiny.

As the seasons shifted and the Faelorian Forest embraced the vibrant hues of autumn, Aidan and Ophelia continued their quest for knowledge and mastery. They had encountered countless wonders and challenges, but the spectre of the Maelthorn lingered in the back of Aidan's mind. The evil creatures remained a constant shadow on the horizon, a reminder that his ultimate purpose was to protect the Phoenix Stone from their insidious grasp.

One evening, as Aidan and Ophelia rested by the banks of a tranquil river, Ophelia spoke of the forest's timeless wisdom. "The Faelorian Forest has endured for countless ages, Aidan, because it embodies the essence of balance. It is a place where the forces of creation and destruction are in constant equilibrium, life emerges from death, and magic flows like a river through the very fabric of existence." Aidan pondered her words, his gaze fixed on the reflection of stars in the river's gentle current. "And I, as the Nura'el, must ensure this balance is maintained?" Ophelia nodded. "Yes, Aidan. Your role is to protect the Phoenix Stone and safeguard the forest's delicate harmony. You are the forest's guardian, its chosen one, and you must wield the Phoenix Stone's power with wisdom and compassion." Ophelia also spoke of the Maelthorn's origins. "The Maelthorn were not always creatures of darkness, Aidan. Long ago, they were beings of magic who dwelled in harmony with the forest. But their greed and ambition led them down a treacherous path, and they sought to harness the Phoenix Stone's power for their purposes." Aidan listened intently, the firelight casting flickering shadows on his face. "Is there any hope for them to return to the path of light?" Ophelia's gaze was sombre. "It is a difficult path, for the darkness that consumes them is not easily dispelled. But there is always hope, Aidan. The forest's magic is a force of renewal, and even the darkest hearts can find redemption."

Their conversation was interrupted by a rustling in the underbrush. Aidan instinctively drew forth the flames of the Phoenix Stone, casting an illuminating glow upon the glade. Emerging from the shadows were not the Maelthorn but a group of forest creatures – foxes, rabbits, and owls – their eyes reflecting curiosity and urgency. One of the owls, a wise old creature with feathers as white as snow, stepped forward and spoke in a voice that resonated with a pearl of timeless wisdom. "Nura'el, we bring grave tidings. The Maelthorns have returned. They have opened a dark portal and capturing the corrupted wellsprings to build another stronghold. Their dark magic once again threatens the balance of the forest." Aidan's heart quickened with a sense of foreboding. "How did this happen? How did they return?" The owl's gaze remained steady. "The forest creatures, ever watchful, had been reporting signs of the Maelthorn's activity. Dark magic had begun to seep into the forest, corrupting once-vibrant groves and twisting the very essence of life. It was a dire warning that the Maelthorn's resurgence was imminent. They have found a source of dark magic, a corrupted wellspring hidden deep within the forest. With its power, they have grown stronger, their malevolence amplified. The Phoenix Stone itself is at risk." Ophelia's expression hardened with resolve. "We cannot allow the Maelthorn to return. Aidan, it is time to confront this threat and protect the Phoenix Stone." Aidan nodded, his eyes aflame with determination. "I will not let the forest fall into darkness. We must find this corrupted wellspring and put an end to it." With a heavy heart, Aidan knew the time for action had come. He stood before the Phoenix Stone, its flames pulsing with an intensity that matched his resolve.

The forest creatures, their trust in Aidan unwavering, pledged their aid in the quest to thwart the Maelthorn's resurgence. They would serve as scouts, guiding him and Ophelia to the location of the corrupted wellspring. As they ventured deeper into the forest, the air grew heavy with a palpable sense of darkness. The once-vibrant foliage became twisted and withered, and the creatures of the forest grew scarce. It was as though the very heart of the forest recoiled from the encroaching malevolence. Days turned into nights, and Aidan's connection to the Phoenix Stone pulsed with a heightened intensity. He could feel the forest's distress, its agony at the corruption that had taken root. The Phoenix Stone's flames burned brightly within him, a beacon of hope amidst the encroaching darkness. They reached the site of the corrupted wellspring. It was a dismal, desolate place, a pool of stagnant water surrounded by gnarled trees and twisted thorns. Dark energy swirled around it, a haze that tainted the very air. Ophelia spoke in hushed tones, her voice tinged with sadness. "This place was once a sacred spring, a well of life's essence. But the Maelthorn have twisted it into a source of corruption." Aidan approached the wellspring, flames flickering in his outstretched hands. He could sense the Phoenix Stone's power surging within him, its flames eager to confront the darkness. With a deep breath, he channelled the Phoenix Stone's energy, directing it toward the corrupted wellspring. The dark energy recoiled and writhed as the flames of the Phoenix Stone clashed with it. It was a battle of opposing forces, a struggle for the soul of the spring. Aidan's determination burned brighter, and he could feel the forest lending strength to his cause. Ophelia joined him, her powers converging with his. Together, they waged a war against the corruption, their flames scorching away the evil magic that had taken root. The forest creatures, watching in awe, added their voices to the chorus of renewal. As the last vestiges of darkness were banished, the corrupted wellspring transformed before their eyes.

The stagnant water became crystal clear, and the surrounding trees began straightening and flourishing. Life returned to the desolate grove, and the air was filled with the melodious songs of birds. Aidan and Ophelia stepped back from the now-purified wellspring, their breaths heavy with exertion. The forest creatures gathered around them, their eyes filled with gratitude. The wise old owl spoke once more, its voice filled with reverence. "You have saved the heart of the forest, Nura'el. The Maelthorn's grip has been weakened." Aidan nodded, a sense of fulfilment washing over him. But he knew that the battle against the Maelthorn was far from over. They would regroup, and their thirst for power would not be easily quenched. Ophelia placed a hand on his shoulder, her eyes filled with pride and concern. "We have won a victory today, Aidan, but the Maelthorn remain a persistent threat. We need to find the dark portal. The forest depends on us." With renewed determination, Aidan gazed at the Phoenix Stone, its flames burning as brightly as ever. With all its secrets and wisdom, the forest awaited his unwavering protection. Aidan and Ophelia continued the search of the dark portal.

One crisp morning, as Aidan and Ophelia stood atop a moss-covered hill, they observed a breathtaking sight – a family of deer, their coats glistening in the morning dew, approaching a serene glade. Aidan felt a deep connection to these creatures, a kinship that transcended words. Ophelia placed a hand on his shoulder, her voice a gentle whisper. "You have become a true guardian of the forest, Aidan. Your bond with its creatures is a testament to the harmony you have forged." Aidan nodded, his heart filled with gratitude. "It is a privilege to be a part of this wondrous tapestry of life." With its ancient wisdom, the forest continued to reveal its secrets to Aidan. Aidan was standing amid a dense grove, his hand resting on the trunk of a towering tree. The tree's gentle and wise spirit spoke to him in a voice that echoed the pain and stress. "Nura'el, you are the forest's heart, the guardian of its magic and the protector of its balance. The forest will become your ally, its inhabitants will serve as scouts and messengers, to find the signs of the Maelthorn's resurgence. But you have to command."

Aidan called upon the forest, converse with them in the language of nature. The forest seemed to sigh with a heavy burden as though it sensed the encroaching darkness. Sensing the situation's urgency, the forest creatures rallied to their cause. Owls became their scouts, eagles their messengers, and foxes their silent guides. Together, they scoured the forest for any signs of the Maelthorn's resurgence, determined to detect their presence before it was too late. Ophelia broke the silence, her voice filled with concern. "The Maelthorn are stirring, Aidan. I can sense their dark portal, like a distant storm on the horizon." Aidan nodded, his gaze fixed on the Phoenix Stone, its flames burning brightly within him. "We cannot allow them to regain their foothold. We must be journey towards the dark portal to confront them."

Ophelia rose to her feet, her eyes filled with determination. "Then let us begin, Aidan. Aidan underwent a meditative state to find the source of the dark portal. Aidan had a vision that transported him to a realm of fire and rebirth. He stood at the edge of a vast, fiery abyss, flames raging around him. But instead of fear, he felt a sense of purpose and determination. In the heart of the inferno, a blazing phoenix soared, its wings a whirlwind of fire and renewal. It circled Aidan, its eyes filled with ancient wisdom, and then descended to merge with him. At that moment, he felt an overwhelming surge of power and clarity, as though he had become one with the phoenix. When he awoke, the memory of the vision burned brightly in his mind. Guided by the forest creatures, Aidan and Ophelia embarked on a journey deep into the forest's heart. The air seemed to crackle with anticipation, as though the forest sensed the impending confrontation. As they reached a clearing bathed in moonlight, they saw the dark portal through which the Maelthorn had returned. It was a swirling vortex of shadow and malice, a tear in the fabric of the forest's magic. Ophelia's voice was resolute. "This is where the Maelthorn draws their power, Aidan. We must close this portal and banish them once and for all." Aidan nodded, flames flickering to life in his outstretched hands. With Ophelia at his side, they advanced toward the portal, determined to confront the darkness that lay beyond.

The ensuing battle was fierce, a clash of elemental forces and willpower. The Maelthorn, their dark forms twisted and contorted, emerged from the portal, their eyes filled with evil intent. But Aidan and Ophelia stood resolute, wielding the Phoenix Stone's power. Flames roared to life, and tendrils of fire danced through the night, clashing with the Maelthorn's dark magic. The forest creatures, loyal allies, joined the fray, their strength bolstering Aidan's resolve. Aidan could feel the Phoenix Stone's flames burning within him as the battle raged on, its power an unyielding force of renewal. With each surge of energy, he pushed back the Maelthorn, dispelling their dark magic and forcing them to retreat.

Finally, as dawn broke over the horizon, the Maelthorn's resistance faltered. With a final burst of flames, Aidan and Ophelia closed the dark portal, sealing the evil creatures within the shadowy abyss from which they had emerged. The forest exhaled a sigh of relief, and the air seemed to shimmer with gratitude. Aidan, his body weary but his spirit resolute, turned to Ophelia. "We have won, Ophelia. The forest is safe." With a smile on her face, Ophelia's eyes gleamed with pride. "You have saved the forest, Aidan, as a guardian and a protector of its balance."

As they returned to their camp beneath Hubert's branches, Aidan couldn't help but feel a profound sense of gratitude for the Faelorian Forest, for Ophelia, and for the Phoenix Stone that had awakened his true potential.

Time flowed like a river through the Faelorian Forest. Aidan's connection to the Phoenix Stone and the forest with each passing season deepened. Under Ophelia's guidance, he continued to hone his abilities, becoming a master of fire and healing. He improved his communication with the forest's creatures, to decipher its secrets, and to understand the delicate balance that sustained its magic. The forest, too, responded to Aidan's presence. It thrived under his watchful gaze, its flora more vibrant, its fauna more abundant. The Phoenix Stone's flames burned with a steady, reassuring light.

As the seasons cycled through their eternal dance, Aidan's reputation as a guardian of the forest continued to grow. But his destiny extended beyond its boundaries, and he was ready to embrace the world with the Phoenix Stone's power as his ally. His journey as a Nura'el continued, and with each step, he carried the forest's magic and wisdom with him, a beacon of hope in a world in need of renewal.

TRIALS OF FIRE

Aidan's unyielding determination blazed even brighter in the aftermath of his harrowing encounter with the Maelthorn, where he heroically sealed the dark portal and emerged victorious as a defender of the Faelorian Forest. Despite this remarkable feat, Aidan remained cognisant that even more significant challenges lay ahead within the forest's depths and beyond its ancient borders.

Aidan's connection with the Phoenix Stone grew ever more robust as time progressed, and he committed himself to mastering its formidable power. Under the wise tutelage of Ophelia, his mentor and guide, Aidan honed his existing skills. He learned advanced techniques and rituals that harnessed the Phoenix Stone's boundless energy. Despite his progress, Aidan remained humble, knowing that much still existed to be uncovered about the Phoenix Stone's true potential.

One evening, as he stood before the Phoenix Stone, its flames casting an ethereal glow, Aidan felt a stirring. It was as though the Phoenix Stone was urging him to explore the uncharted territories of its magic.

Ophelia noticed the contemplative look on his face and approached him. "What weighs on your mind, Aidan?"

Aidan turned to her, his eyes filled with curiosity and determination. "I believe there's more to the Phoenix Stone's power than we've uncovered. I can feel its energy calling to me, as though it has secrets waiting to be revealed."

Ophelia regarded him with a thoughtful expression. "The Phoenix Stone is a wellspring of ancient magic, and its depths are unfathomable. If you feel a connection to its hidden potential, perhaps it is time to embark on a journey of discovery."

Aidan nodded, the flames of the Phoenix Stone's fire dancing with anticipation. "I will heed its call and seek to unlock its mysteries."

With an unwavering trust in his instincts, Aidan embarked on a journey into the heart of the Faelorian Forest. Guided by the harmonious melodies of the creatures and the towering trees, he found himself standing at the entrance of the Veiled Grove. This secluded clearing was renowned for its powerful magic and mythical status, and Aidan felt the palpable energy of the Phoenix Stone's influence vibrating through the surrounding flora and fauna. The boundaries between the mortal and mystical realms were blurred, and Aidan was humbled to be in the presence of such otherworldly power. As he stepped into the clearing, a gentle, enchanting light greeted Aidan, and the ancient trees that encircled him were adorned with glowing moss and ivy. His eyes were immediately drawn to the twisted oak tree, etched with cryptic symbols and runes that stood at the centre of it all. Aidan knew in his heart that this tree held the key to unlocking the Phoenix Stone's hidden potential, and he prepared himself to delve deeper into the grove's mysteries.

With a deep breath, he approached the ancient oak and placed his hand on its weathered bark. The moment his palm touched the tree's surface, energy coursed through him. It was as though the tree was welcoming him, acknowledging his presence. As Aidan closed his eyes and focused, he began to feel a resonance between himself, the Phoenix Stone, and the ancient oak. It was a symphony of magic, each note harmonising with the others, creating a tapestry of power that pulsed through him. He whispered words of gratitude to the tree spirit, and in response, the runes on the oak's trunk began to glow with an inner light. Symbols and patterns emerged, each representing a facet of the Phoenix Stone's magic. Aidan realised this was a language of the forest, a key to unlocking his sought secrets.

Days turned into nights as Aidan immersed himself in his studies within the Veiled Grove. He learned to communicate with the ancient tree spirit, which identified itself as Elindor, the guardian of the grove. Elindor shared stories of the Phoenix Stone's creation and the rituals of the forest's druidic past. Under Elindor's guidance, Aidan delved into the Phoenix Stone's energy with newfound understanding. He discovered that the Phoenix Stone was not merely a source of fire and healing but a conduit to the heart of the forest's magic. It held the power to manipulate the elements, to control the weather, and to commune with the spirits of the land. As Aidan stood in the Veiled Grove, he looked up at the starry sky and focused on channelling the Phoenix Stone's energy. The stars responded by intensifying their light and dancing in intricate patterns. Elindor's voice whispered in his mind, telling him about the new facet of the Phoenix Stone's magic - the power of the stars, a connection to the celestial realms. Aidan realised that the Phoenix Stone's power was limitless, bound only by his imagination and understanding. He was excited to share his discoveries with Ophelia and show her the untapped potential of the Phoenix Stone. Before leaving, Aidan felt a disturbance in the forest. The air vibrated with tension, and the trees whispered of an encroaching darkness. With a sense of foreboding, Aidan followed the feeling, his instincts guiding him deeper into the forest. Soon, he stumbled upon a scene that sent a shiver down his spine.

A group of forest creatures – foxes, rabbits, and owls – stood huddled together in fear. Before them, a menacing figure loomed. It was a creature of shadow and malice, its eyes gleaming with malevolence. It was not the Maelthorn but a lesser foe, a creature drawn by the allure of the Phoenix Stone's magic. Its form fluid and ever shifting, making it nearly impossible to discern its true shape. Its eyes burn with evil, and its tendrils of darkness writhe like serpents. Its malevolent intent was clear, and Aidan knew he could not allow it to harm the forest or its inhabitants.

The creature hissed, its voice a sinister whisper. "I sense the power of the Phoenix Stone within you, Nura'el. Hand it over, and perhaps I will spare these creatures." Aidan's heart pounded as he faced his first true challenge. He glanced at the trembling forest creatures, their eyes filled with fear. With a determined voice, he responded to the shadowy figure. "I will not surrender the Phoenix Stone to darkness. I will defend it with all my strength." The creature's form wavered and shifted as though considering its options. Then, with a chilling laughter, it lunged at Aidan, its dark magic crackling in the air. The battle ensued was a test of Aidan's abilities as a Nura'el. He summoned flames that blazed with the intensity of the Phoenix Stone's power, using them to ward off the creature's attacks. The creature's attacks are swift and unpredictable, its shadowy tendrils striking out with lethal precision.

Each clash of magic sent sparks flying, casting eerie shadows in the moonlit forest. Aidan's heart raced with adrenaline as the battle raged on, and he quickly realised that his opponent was no ordinary creature. It possessed a cunning intellect, allowing it to evade his flames easily. Aidan knew that he had to stay focused and determined if he wanted to overcome this shadowy foe. He refused to back down or yield to its evil presence. The battle raged on, the forest seeming to respond to the clash of opposing forces. Trees sway and whisper secrets of ancient magic, and the air crackles with energy. It became clear that this battle isn't just physical but a trials of wills and powers beyond mortal comprehension. Aidan closed his eyes, his mind filled with visions of phoenixes soaring through the skies, their fiery feathers ablaze. He knew that this was the celestial power he had to seek. It was key to defeating the shadowy creature. With a surge of energy, Aidan channelled the power of the Phoenix Stone, invoking the stars above. The celestial energy coalesced into a radiant sphere that he hurled at the shadowy creature. The moment the divine magic enveloped it, the shadowy foe cried out in agony, unable to withstand the power of the Phoenix Stone. The forest creatures watched in awe as the beast dissipated into nothingness, leaving only the echoes of its evil presence behind.

Aidan stood victorious, his chest heaving with exertion but his spirit unbroken. The forest creatures, who had been afraid, approached him with gratitude. The wise old owl, their spokesman, spoke reverently, acknowledging Aidan's bravery and skill. "You have protected the forest again, Nura'el," he said. "We are grateful for your presence." As he reflected on his accomplishments, Aidan experienced a surge of pride and satisfaction. He knew that he had done the right thing and had once again been able to defend the forest against those seeking to harm it. Aidan looked up at the stars with a smile, feeling their energy still coursing through his veins. He knew he would always be ready to defend the forest, no matter the challenges. Aidan nodded, his gaze shifting to the Phoenix Stone, which pulsed with approval. It reminded him that his journey was far from over, that the forest's magic was a wellspring of challenges and discoveries. As the celestial power flowed through Aidan, he made a solemn vow to use it wisely and protect the world from evil.

With the forest creatures as his witnesses and the power of the cosmos at his side, Aidan departed from the Veiled Grove. His heart filled with a sense of accomplishment. He knew that this minor foe was a glimpse of the trials he would face in the future, but he was prepared to confront them all. As he returned to Ophelia, he couldn't help but smile. The Phoenix Stone's power was boundless, and his connection to it grew stronger each day. He was ready to embrace his destiny as a Nura'el, a guardian of the forest and a protector of its magic, with unwavering determination and a heart ablaze with hope.

LEGACY OF THE PHOENIX CLAN

To understand the Nura'els and their deep-rooted connection to the legendary Phoenix, one must journey back to an era when the world was a realm of untamed magic and mythical beings. Long before the advent of recorded history, the ancient days were characterised by elemental chaos, where the elements of fire, water, earth, and air intermingled in a ceaseless dance, giving rise to powerful and capricious forces. Among these forces was the mythical creature, the Phoenix, a magnificent being born of fire and rebirth. The Phoenix represented renewal and resurrection, a creature of unparalleled beauty and power. Its feathers shimmered with iridescent hues, its wings spanned the horizon, and its song could soothe even the most troubled souls. However, the most remarkable aspect of the Phoenix was its ability to be consumed by flames and rise from its ashes, reborn and more glorious than before. This astounding ability was attributed to the Phoenix's innate connection to the element of fire, which granted it the power to transcend death and emerge anew, a symbol of hope and renewal in a world rife with chaos and destruction.

The legends spoke of the Phoenix as a guardian of the elemental balance, a being tasked with maintaining harmony in a world that teetered on the brink of chaos. It was said that the Phoenix could harness the primal forces of fire and healing, using its power to mend the world's wounds and restore life to barren lands. As time passed, the existence of the Phoenix became shrouded in myth and mystery. Its appearances grew increasingly rare, and its role as a guardian of the elemental balance faded from the world's collective memory. But the Phoenix's essence endured, its magic sleeping within the world's heart, waiting for the right moment to awaken.

A young warrior named Thalion emerged during the Age of Legends when mortals and mystical beings coexisted. He had an unyielding spirit and insatiable curiosity and was inspired by tales of the Phoenix from his elders. Thalion embarked on a perilous quest to seek out the legendary creature of fire and rebirth that held the power to heal the world. Thalion learned to harness the primal forces of fire and healing with guidance from the enigmatic druids. He communed with the elements, mastered the art of fire manipulation, and delved into the mysteries of magic. In a sacred grove hidden deep within the forest, Thalion encountered the Phoenix for the first time. Its presence was awe-inspiring, its flames a blaze of ethereal beauty. The Phoenix regarded Thalion with eyes that seemed to hold the wisdom of the ages. Thalion approached the awe-inspiring Phoenix with utmost humility and respect, its fiery plumage radiating mystical energy. He tentatively extended his hand, scarcely daring to hope to be granted the privilege of touching such a magnificent creature. To his utter amazement, the Phoenix allowed him to make contact with its feathers, and in that moment, a deep connection was formed. Thalion could feel the Phoenix's ancient magic coursing through him, its essence merging with his own being. Overwhelmed by this incredible experience, Thalion returned to the druidic order, his newfound powers a testament to his bond with the Phoenix. He had become the first of an esteemed lineage of protectors known as the Nura'els, entrusted with maintaining the delicate balance of the elements and utilising the Phoenix's powerful magic to serve the greater good.

Led by the wise and capable Thalion, the Nura'els flourished over the years, with new members being initiated into their ranks and taught the secrets of their powers. These skilled fighters became the guardians of the natural world, utilising their unique abilities to restore balance to a world constantly on the brink of destruction. From healing the land to protecting the forests, the Nura'els were tireless in preserving the planet's delicate harmony. With the time, the world underwent significant transformations. The primal forces that used to dominate gradually weakened, and the mystical creatures that once roamed the lands became scarce. Even the Phoenix, a majestic creature, became a rare sight, withdrawing into the depths of the world, its magic dormant and waiting for a time when it was needed once more. The Nura'els' lineage endured, but their powers dwindled, mirroring the fading magic of the world. They became the guardians of a forgotten legacy, protectors of ancient traditions, and stewards of the last remaining embers of the Phoenix's magic.

In the midst of great turmoil, a momentous event known as "The Collapse" forever altered the balance of the world. Once held in check, the elemental forces surged back with a renewed sense of chaos, causing forests to wither, seas to rage, and skies to darken with storms. And yet, amidst this chaos, a new hero emerged: Althea, a young and determined warrior who, like Thalion before her, felt the call of the Phoenix's magic deep within her soul. With a fierce determination, Althea stepped forward to face the challenges ahead, ready to take on any obstacle in her path.

As she journeyed through the vast expanse of the Faelorian Forest, Althea's heart was set on reaching its centre. In this place, the balance of elemental forces was at its most fragile and where she hoped to uncover the remains of the once-powerful Phoenix. And so, with unwavering determination, Althea pushed forward. As she arrived at the forest's centre, Althea's eyes fell upon a faint flame, the remnants of the Phoenix's former glory. She knew then that she had to act swiftly if there was any hope of restoring the elemental balance and rekindling the Phoenix's magic. In her quest for knowledge, Althea turned to the ancient tree spirit Hubert for guidance. Through him, she learned about the Phoenix's true nature and the legacy of the Nura'els. But it was when Hubert revealed the existence of the Phoenix Stone. This mystical artefact was the key to unlocking the Phoenix's magic: Althea knew she was on the right path. With Hubert's words echoing in her mind, Althea set out on a new journey that would take her deeper into the forest's heart than she had ever gone. For the first time, she felt a glimmer of hope that the Phoenix's magic might be restored and the balance of elemental forces that the world desperately needed.

The Phoenix Stone was said to be a fragment of the Phoenix's essence, a source of fire and healing that could rekindle the world's magic. It was a relic of immense power, hidden within the Faelorian Forest, waiting for a Nura'el to claim it. With Hubert's guidance, Althea embarked on a dangerous quest to find the Phoenix Stone. Along the way, she encountered challenges and adversaries, each testing her resolve and mastery of fire and healing. Finally, after a series of trials and tribulations, Althea stood before the Phoenix Stone, a gem of fiery brilliance that pulsed with the Phoenix's magic. She touched the Phoenix Stone with reverence, forging a connection that transcended time and space. At that moment, the Phoenix's magic awakened within her, and she became the precursor of renewal. The elemental forces responded to her call, the forests flourished, the seas calmed, and the skies cleared. The world began to heal, and the balance was restored. Althea's actions saved the world from impending chaos and rekindled the legacy of the Nura'els. Under her leadership, a new generation of protectors emerged, each bearing the mark of the Phoenix and the power of the Phoenix Stone. The Nura'els continued their mission, safeguarding the elemental balance and using the Phoenix's magic to heal the world's wounds. They became beacons of hope, guardians of the natural world, and champions of renewal.

As the ages passed, the Nura'els' powers continued to evolve. They learned to commune with the forest's creatures, decipher nature's secrets, and protect the Faelorian Forest from the encroaching darkness of the Maelthorn. The Maelthorn were an evil force that sought to corrupt the Phoenix Stone's magic and plunge the world into eternal darkness. They were drawn to the Phoenix Stone's power like moths to a flame, and the Nura'els became their greatest adversaries. Generations of Nura'els confronted the Maelthorn, waging a relentless war to protect the Phoenix Stone and the elemental balance. They faced formidable challenges, battled dark sorcery, and endured hardships that tested their resolve. But the legacy of the Nura'els took, their determination fueled by the knowledge that they were the last defenders of the Phoenix's magic. They stood as a bulwark against the chaos that threatened to engulf the world, their flames burning bright with hope and renewal.

In the modern era, Aidan had emerged as the latest in the line of Nura'els. His connection to the Phoenix Stone and the legendary Phoenix ran deep, and he had proven himself as a guardian of the Faelorian Forest and a protector of the elemental balance. However, his challenges were more expansive than the forest's boundaries. The world beyond beckoned, a realm in need of the Phoenix's magic and the legacy of the Nura'els. Aidan's journey was far from over, and the destiny of the Nura'els was entwined with the world's fate. As Aidan gazed at the Phoenix Stone, its flames burning brightly within him, he knew that he carried the weight of history on his shoulders. The legacy of the Nura'els was a beacon of hope in a world threatened by darkness, and he was prepared to embrace his role with unwavering determination and a heart ablaze with the Phoenix's magic.

As Aidan continued his journey as a Nura'el, his connection to the Phoenix Stone and the legendary Phoenix deepened. He had learned of the ancient history of his lineage and the profound duty that came with it. Yet, mysteries and prophecies remained that eluded him, secrets buried within the annals of time.

One fateful evening, as Aidan and Ophelia sat beneath the ancient oak tree, Hubert, they were joined by a venerable visitor—a sage named Eldric. Eldric was a scholar of ancient lore and a keeper of prophecies, and his arrival heralded a momentous revelation. Eldric greeted them with a knowing smile, his eyes twinkling with wisdom. "Nura'el Aidan, Ophelia, I have journeyed from afar to share a great significance prophecy passed down through the ages." Intrigued, Aidan and Ophelia exchanged glances, their curiosity piqued. They gestured for Eldric to continue, eager to hear the prophecy that had brought him to the heart of the Faelorian Forest.

Eldric cleared his throat and began to recite the prophecy in a voice that seemed to carry the weight of centuries:

As the Phoenix Stone's flame burns bright,
And the Phoenix's magic takes flight,
A chosen one with great power,
Shall rise to confront the darkness, never to cower.

They will have the gift of fire and healing,
A protector of the world whose strength is revealing.
Their journey begins in the heart of the woods,
To mend all that's broken and heal all that's not good.

But there's a grander quest beyond the trees,
To rekindle hope and face all unease.
The Phoenix's light is what the world awaits,
To banish the shadows and end all the hates.

Together in unity and purpose, they'll stand,
The Nura'el, a guiding hand.
With the Phoenix Stone's power, balance will be restored,
Ending all the evil, fulfilling the legacy adored.

As Eldric concluded the prophecy, a hush fell over the ancient oak grove. The words hung in the air, their significance sinking in. Aidan and Ophelia exchanged solemn glances, realising the magnitude of the prophecy and its implications. Eldric spoke once more, his voice filled with gravitas. "The time has come, Nura'el Aidan. The prophecy speaks of your destiny and the destiny of all Nura'els who have come before you. The world needs the Phoenix's light, and you are the chosen one to carry that torch."

Aidan nodded, a sense of purpose burning within him. "I accept this destiny, Eldric. I will do whatever it takes to fulfil the prophecy and protect the world from darkness." Ophelia's eyes filled with determination, and she added, "We stand with Aidan, Eldric. Together, we will restore the balance and rekindle hope." Eldric smiled, his presence radiating reassurance. "The path ahead will not be without challenges, but the legacy of the Nura'els is a testament to the indomitable spirit of renewal. The world awaits your guidance, Nura'el Aidan, and the Phoenix's magic shall guide your way."

With the prophecy unveiling, Aidan's journey took on a new dimension. His destiny was now intricately linked with the world's fate, and he carried the weight of the Phoenix's legacy. But with the Phoenix Stone's power and the wisdom of the forest as his allies, he was prepared to face the trials ahead and rekindle hope in a world yearning for renewal.

In the wake of the prophecy's revelation, Aidan's resolve to fulfil his destiny as a Nura'el burned brighter than ever. He knew that the world awaited the Phoenix's light, and he was determined to rise to the challenge. But he also understood that he could not embark on this journey alone. Aidan felt a calling deep within him—a yearning to seek out other guardians who shared their purpose. He believed unity and cooperation would be essential in facing the looming darkness.

EMBER OF FRIENDSHIP

Aidan and Ophelia, two brave souls, had embarked on an epic quest beyond the confines of their woodland home in the sprawling Faelorian Forest. As they journeyed forth, the enigmatic Phoenix Stone guided them, and their spirits were inspired by the profound legacy of the Nura'els. Their mission was to unite with fellow guardians who shared their purpose and work together towards a common goal. They ventured beyond the forest's borders, they traversed distant lands and uncharted waters, driven by their unwavering determination to fulfil the prophecy and rekindle hope in a world shrouded in darkness. Their ultimate objective was to find kindred spirits who could aid them in their noble quest, and together, they would strive to bring light to a world that desperately needed it.

Aidan and Ophelia embarked on a daunting quest to unravel the true power of the Tideheart, an awe-inspiring body of water rumoured to hold the mysteries of the vast seas. The duo found themselves on the enigmatic island of Aquaria, a place far removed from their familiar world, where the magic of the elements was at its most potent. On this mystical island, they encountered Lirael, an extraordinary water mage whose exceptional talent was unparalleled in its magnitude. Lirael, with her adept ability to manipulate water's power, was a formidable force and a protector of the intricate equilibrium between various elemental forces. Her profound understanding of the significance of the quest at hand led her to make an unwavering decision to join Aidan and Ophelia in their pursuit. Together, they draw upon the Tideheart's mystical energies

33

and harness the profound power of elemental forces. As the group called out to the Tideheart, the previously calm and still pool of water suddenly transformed into a bustling and thriving hub of marine life. It was a mesmerising sight to behold as the sea around them became tranquil, and its vitality surged with energy. This was a momentous occasion for the group as their bond was forged in the heart of the ocean. Lirael, with her extensive knowledge of water magic and unwavering dedication to their shared purpose, played a crucial role in making this happen. Her contribution cemented her place in the fellowship as they set forth from Aquaria, enriched by their newfound knowledge and strengthened by their shared experience.

As their quest progressed, Aidan, Ophelia, and Lirael found themselves journeying towards the secluded Solara Peak. In this mountain sanctuary, a community of monks revered the elemental forces of air and fire. They hoped to discover a guardian who could assist them in unlocking the breath of renewal, a power they believed was crucial to achieving their ultimate goal. Upon arriving at the monastery, the trio were introduced to Kaelen, a monk whose mastery of windshaper was unparalleled. Kaelen was a guardian of the elemental balance and had long been drawn to the mission that Aidan, Ophelia and Lirael seek. Recognising the importance and urgency of their quest, he offered his expertise and knowledge to their cause, eager to help them achieve their objective. Kaelen's proficiency was not solely a display of his innate elemental abilities but a testament to his unyielding dedication to their joint mission. Their connection grew stronger as they synchronised their powers within the Solarium. In this very place, Aidan and Kaleen intersected the elemental forces of air and fire. Flames flickered with newfound vigour while the radiance of sunlight obliterated all traces of darkness as they channelled the magic of Solara Peak, effectively piercing through the heavens. The fellowship's mission was greatly enhanced with the addition of Kaelen, a steadfast guardian who proved to be an invaluable asset. Kaelen's unrelenting determination and loyalty served as a beacon of inspiration to all who were fortunate enough to have him by their side. His inclusion in the group added depth and complexity, enriching their overall dynamic. As an elemental force of air,

Kaelen's presence was felt by all, infusing the group with a renewed sense of purpose and energy.

Following Aidan's expedition to Solara Peak, they were joined by Nalorin, the guardian of the earth. His mastery over the earth realm was unlike any other, enabling him to easily control the ground, mountain and volcanoes. This made him an invaluable addition to their team as they pursued their goal of restoring balance to the elements. It was unmistakable that Nalorin held an unwavering commitment to revitalising the earth. His profound connection with the ebb and flow of the earth spoke volumes about his dedication to the cause. His bond with the elemental equilibrium ran as deep as the vast expanses of the earth itself, and this understanding gave him a unique perspective on the urgency of their mission. Nalorin recognised their critical role in restoring the natural order, and he approached his work with steadfast determination and an unwavering sense of purpose. Nalorin loomed over the group, constantly reminding them of their vital responsibility. The bond between Aidan, Ophelia, Lirael, Kaelen and Nalorin grew ever stronger, cementing Nalorin's position as a stalwart defender of the earth.

During the course of Aidan's journey, Ophelia, the young and revered spirit of the forest, remained a constant and unwavering presence. She was more than a mere mentor to Aidan; she was a loyal companion on his quest. Ophelia's guidance and sagacity were a wellspring of fortitude, and her link with Aidan was profound, anchored in their mutual responsibility to safeguard the Phoenix Stone and the Faelorian Forest. Ophelia's contributions to the group went beyond that of a mere mentor. She was a protector and custodian of the forest, and her deep-rooted connection to the natural world was unparalleled. Ophelia's wisdom and expertise on the magic of the Phoenix Stone were invaluable assets to the group, providing them with insightful guidance on harnessing the elemental forces they sought to control. Her presence was a source of enrichment to the fellowship, serving as a bridge between the ancient wisdom of the forest and their own efforts to understand and harness the powerful forces of nature. The connections between them were not mere alliances but rather unbreakable bonds of destiny forged through a mutual dedication to restoring the balance of the elements.

Each member brought their distinct abilities and perspectives to the table, which, when combined, created a fellowship that exceeded the sum of its individual parts. Such was the power and harmony of their shared purpose that it propelled them towards success in their quest. As they continued on their path, the fellowship members found that their group grew closer, and their relationships became stronger. Every individual was united by a shared goal: to fulfil the prophecy, restore the balance of the elements, and bring renewed faith to a world under siege from the forces of darkness.

Embarking on a journey brimming with opportunities and promise, our intrepid adventurers were prepared to venture through uncharted lands, discovering long-forgotten enigmas and facing trials that surpass even their most imaginative thoughts. Led by the mystical energies of the Phoenix Stone and inspired by the legendary heritage of the Nura'els, they were ready and prepared to face any challenge that may arise on their journey.

The fellowship formed among them was not merely a collection of individuals but a reflection of the remarkable strength and potential that can be unleashed through unity and cooperation in the face of challenges. As they pressed on with their shared mission, their interconnectedness and shared destiny will become a source of unwavering support and encouragement, allowing them to overcome the obstacles and hardships ahead and ultimately find the fulfilment they sought.

THE ECLIPSE SYNDICATE

In the vast expanse of the cosmic tapestry, where celestial bodies collided, and stars were born, it's concerning to know that there exist enclaves of darkness called "The Whispers of Darkness". These are remnants of the evil forces that once threatened the universe with their nefarious ambitions. They are pockets of shadow and malice that linger in the universe, always present yet never entirely subdued. Their insidious whispers hold the power to tempt those who are susceptible to their influence, seeking to disrupt the delicate cosmic balance that the Nura'els have tirelessly worked to preserve. The evil whispers pose a constant threat to the harmony of the universe, and their presence cannot be ignored. These whispers are a force to be reckoned with, and the vigilance of all who seek to maintain balance in the universe must remain steadfast to keep them at bay.

Aidan and his fellowship, guided by Ophelia's cosmic wisdom, were tasked with confronting these lingering threats. Their unity remained their greatest strength, as they understood that the forces of darkness could only be defeated through the unwavering commitment to cosmic order and the selflessness that had defined their journey. As the cosmic guardians continued their watchful vigil, they encountered these pockets of darkness, each presenting a unique challenge. The Whispers of Darkness sought to corrupt cosmic energies, disrupt the balance, and sow discord among the universe's inhabitants. In these cosmic battles against the Whispers of Darkness, the Nura'els continued to evolve, deepening their understanding of the universe's intricate web of energies and forces. Each confrontation was a test of their resolve, a reminder that their mission was eternal, and the cosmic harmony they protected was a fragile tapestry that required constant vigilance. As they faced these challenges, their bond as cosmic guardians grew stronger, and their legacy continued to inspire those who followed in their footsteps. The Whispers of Darkness were a reminder that the universe's balance was a perpetual struggle. Still, the Nura'els remained steadfast in their commitment to uphold the cosmic order for the benefit of all beings across the cosmos.

Aidan and his fellowship of guardians persevered on their journey to fulfil the ancient prophecy and re-establish the natural harmony of the elements. However, they were soon confronted with a daunting challenge that would challenge their loyalty and faith in one another. Unknown to them, a shadowy and nefarious organisation known as the "Eclipse Syndicate" had closely observed their every move. The organisation was enticed by the potential to exploit the Phoenix Stone's power and the legendary Phoenix's formidable magic for their malicious agenda. The Eclipse Syndicate was a covert organisation that had long been fixated on manipulating the forces of nature to serve their selfish ends. Led by a mysterious figure who went by the name "Shadowveil," this nefarious group had managed to infiltrate various corners of the world, spreading their influence like tendrils of darkness. Shadowveil was a master of shadow magic and manipulation, possessing a cunning intellect and an insatiable thirst for power. He had become aware of Aidan's fellowship and recognised the Phoenix Stone's magic's potential to further his goals. Operating from the shadows, the Eclipse Syndicate had taken great pains to gather information on Aidan's journey, tracking the locations of the elemental sources they sought to control. Their spies, shrouded in secrecy and cloaked in darkness, watched as Aidan, Ophelia, Lirael, Kaelen, and Nalorin harnessed the elemental magic and performed acts of renewal. The syndicate was convinced that the guardians were merely pawns in a larger game, unwittingly gathering the knowledge and power Shadowveil needed to achieve his ultimate objective—to unlock the Phoenix's magic and bend it to his will. This would allow him to become the supreme master of the elements and further his plans for domination.

As Aidan and his fellowship continued their journey, the signs of interference became increasingly apparent. Mysterious disruptions, unexplained magical anomalies, and unsettling encounters with shadowy figures marred the delicate balance of elemental forces they sought to restore. It was as if a web of deceit had been woven around their mission, seeking to obscure their path and thwart their cosmic purpose.

One of the most significant encounters occurred during their visit to the ancient Elemental Library—a revered repository of knowledge about the world's elemental forces. Within the hallowed halls of the library, scrolls and tomes dating back millennia held the secrets of elemental magic, including the ancient and powerful spell of the Phoenix. Here, Aidan and his fellowship first crossed paths with members of the enigmatic Eclipse Syndicate. These infiltrators, cloaked in the guise of scholars and seekers of elemental wisdom, had a nefarious agenda. Their objective was to pilfer valuable tomes, artefacts, and relics that held the key to unlocking the dormant magic of the Phoenix. A confrontation of epic proportions unfolded within the sacred confines of the Elemental Library. Spells clashed, elemental forces surged, and the very foundations of the library trembled with the intensity of the struggle between light and shadow. It was a battle of raw magical power and cosmic principles—the enduring light of the Nura'els against the insidious darkness of the Eclipse Syndicate. Ultimately, the intruders were driven off, their nefarious mission thwarted. However, they left behind a trail of cryptic symbols and clues that hinted at the true extent of the Eclipse Syndicate's involvement. These symbols were like threads woven into the cosmic tapestry, revealing that the web of deceit extended far beyond the Elemental Library. As Aidan and his fellowship delved deeper into the mystery of the Eclipse Syndicate, they realised that they were confronting a shadowy organisation with designs that spanned the cosmos. Their mission to restore the balance of elemental forces had cosmic implications and profound consequences for the ongoing battle against the forces of darkness.

This encounter marked the beginning of a relentless pursuit. This cosmic cat-and-mouse game would take them to the universe's farthest reaches in their quest to unravel the web of deceit and confront the true architects of the Eclipse Syndicate. With each step, they were drawn further into a cosmic conflict that would test their mettle and reshape the very destiny of the Nura'els.

Following their unsettling encounter in the Elemental Library, Aidan and his companions found themselves grappling with a deep sense of doubt and suspicion. The enigmatic Eclipse Syndicate's presence had shaken the foundations of their trust, casting a long shadow over their cosmic quest to restore the elemental balance. As they journeyed through treacherous terrain, the Nura'els discovered that trust had become a precious commodity, with the boundaries between allies and adversaries blurred. The true intentions of those they encountered remained veiled in shadows, leaving them to navigate a path fraught with uncertainty.

Perhaps the most disheartening discovery was the existence of other guardians, individuals who had once fought alongside them in the cosmic struggle against darkness but had now fallen prey to the cunning manipulations of the Eclipse Syndicate. These once-trusted allies had been deceived, coerced, or ensnared by the syndicate's web of lies, and they now served the dark agenda with a fervour that bordered on fanaticism. When Aidan and his fellowship encountered these former companions, the pain of betrayal cut deep. The twisted influence of the syndicate had transformed them into physical adversaries, attacking with a ferocity born of desperation and the weight of their manipulated loyalties. The battle was against external foes, the perversion of trust and the erosion of the cosmic bonds that had once united them. The bonds of destiny, which had served as an unbreakable force of unity among the Nura'els, were now strained to their limits. Realising that not everyone could be trusted left them with a profound sense of isolation and vulnerability. Deception had taken root in the most unexpected places, and the cosmic struggle against darkness had become a battle against external foes and the erosion of trust within their heavenly family.

Yet, amidst the trials and tribulations, Aidan and his companions clung to the core principles that had guided them from the beginning—the unwavering commitment to cosmic order, the enduring light of the Phoenix Stone, and the belief that, ultimately, trust and unity would prevail over the forces of deception and darkness. Their resolve remained unshaken, for they understood that their cosmic journey was a test not only of their powers but also of the strength of their heavenly bonds and the resilience of their trust in the face of betrayal. In the unravelling of trust, the Nura'els discovered a profound truth—that the greatest test of faith often occurred when trust was most fragile and that the bonds of destiny were most potent when tested against the forces of darkness. The cosmic struggle against the Eclipse Syndicate was far from over, and Aidan and his companions were determined to confront not only external adversaries but also the internal doubts and uncertainties that threatened to undermine their cosmic mission.

Aidan and his companions journeyed ahead and encountered "The Whispering Caves". A labyrinthine network of subterranean tunnels hidden deep within the world, beckoned Aidan and his companions on their quest to restore the elemental balance. These caves were steeped in myth and legend, rumoured to hold the long-forgotten secrets of the world's elemental forces. It was here, in the heart of the subterranean labyrinth, that they would make an ominous revelation—a revelation that would lay bare the true extent of the Eclipse Syndicate's involvement and the chilling depth of Shadowveil's ambitions. As they ventured deeper into the Whispering Caves, the air grew heavy with an eerie stillness, and the walls seemed to whisper ancient secrets. The earth beneath their feet resonated with a primal energy hinting at the elemental forces that had shaped the world since immemorial. Their journey through the winding tunnels eventually led them to a hidden chamber—an arcane sanctum cloaked in darkness. The chamber's walls were adorned with intricate diagrams and inscriptions, each one a piece of a sinister puzzle. These cryptic markings detailed the syndicate's grand plan, a plan that sent shivers down their spines.

Shadowveil, the enigmatic mastermind behind the Eclipse Syndicate, harboured nothing short of apocalyptic ambitions. The revelation in the hidden chamber laid bare the depths of his evil scheme. He sought to converge the elemental forces—fire, water, air, and earth—into a singular source of unimaginable power, a source that he believed could rival the very magic of the Phoenix Stone itself. This dark ritual, if completed, would serve a dual purpose for the syndicate. It would grant them dominion over the elemental forces, allowing them to control and manipulate these primal energies. Yet, the consequences of this ritual extended far beyond the realm of personal power. The convergence of the elemental forces would unleash chaos and devastation upon the world, shattering the delicate balance that had existed for aeons. The elemental equilibrium, which Aidan and his fellowship had strived so tirelessly to restore, would be shattered, and the world would be plunged into an era of darkness and despair. The foundations of the natural order would crumble, and the world as they knew it would be irrevocably altered. The weight of this ominous revelation hung heavy in the chamber, a chilling reminder of the stakes at hand. Aidan and his steadfast fellowship understood that they were not only battling against the Eclipse Syndicate but also against the cataclysmic forces of elemental convergence that threatened to engulf their world in darkness. With newfound determination, they knew that their mission had taken on an even greater significance—a cosmic battle to protect the elemental balance and prevent the world's descent into chaos and devastation at the hands of the syndicate's insidious ambitions.

Armed with the knowledge of the syndicate's apocalyptic ambitions, they understood that the moment had come to confront their shadowy adversaries and halt the cataclysmic convergence of elemental forces that Shadowveil sought to unleash upon the world. The bonds of destiny that had united them were put to the ultimate test as they readied themselves for the impending showdown. The stage for the final confrontation was set in the heart of the Faelorian Forest, where the Phoenix Stone pulsed with renewed vigour and cosmic energy. It was here, amidst the ancient trees and the radiant presence of the Phoenix Stone that the Nura'els would face off against the Eclipse Syndicate. The syndicate, bolstered by their stolen elemental artefacts and mastery of dark shadow magic, stood ready to defend their evil agenda. Their ranks included formidable adversaries manipulated into serving their dark cause.

Aidan, Ophelia, Lirael, Kaelen and Nalorin stood resolute on the opposing side. Their powers, honed by years of cosmic trials, were formidable. Still, their unity and unbreakable bonds of destiny would ultimately prove their greatest strength. The clash of cosmic forces was nothing short of spectacular. Spells and incantations filled the air, elemental energies clashed with shadowy darkness, and the forest seemed to hold its breath as the battle raged on. The stakes were clear—the world's fate hung in the balance, and the outcome of this cosmic struggle would determine whether the elemental equilibrium would be preserved or shattered. Ultimately, it was not just the elemental mastery and sheer power of Aidan and his fellowship that prevailed. It was their unwavering unity, shared purpose, and indomitable belief in the cosmic order they protected. Together, they thwarted Shadowveil's dark ritual, scattering the elemental forces and preventing the catastrophic convergence that would have plunged the world into chaos.

The Eclipse Syndicate dealt a severe blow, saw its members captured, and its nefarious influence shattered. However, Shadowveil, the enigmatic mastermind behind the syndicate's sinister designs, managed to elude capture, vanishing into the depths of the Faelorian Forest. He vowed vengeance and promised a return in a future, more insidious form, leaving an unsettling air of uncertainty in his wake.

As the dust settled and the echoes of battle faded, Aidan and his companions understood that the immediate threat of the Eclipse Syndicate had been temporarily thwarted. Yet, they were acutely aware that the shadows of deception still lingered, and the cosmic struggle against darkness was an ongoing journey. Their path continued, illuminated by the radiant presence of the Phoenix Stone and guided by the unwavering bonds of destiny that held them together. The world was in need of the Phoenix's light, and they were determined to carry it forward, no matter what cosmic challenges awaited on the horizon.

ASCENSION

In a world veiled in mystery and magic, Aidan continued his journey with his faithful companions. Their mission to bring balance back to the elemental world became more arduous with each passing challenge. The enemies they encountered were formidable, testing the limits of the guardians' capabilities. Nevertheless, Aidan's proficiency in wielding his Nura'el abilities continued to flourish with every obstacle they faced, allowing him to access the uncharted depths of his power. Aidan's destiny unfolded before him, a destiny entwined with the names of three formidable foes – Pyrrhia, the enigmatic sorceress; Tempestia, the sorceress of storms; and Abyssalon, the dark lord of abyss.

Aidan's initial confrontation with a formidable opponent transpired within the very core of the treacherous Strudderion, a realm where elemental forces perpetually collided in a tumultuous dance and pernicious entities thrived. Within this realm, the equilibrium of elemental forces was at its most precarious, and the potency of the Phoenix's mystical power seemed to diminish, constantly tested by the unyielding turbulence. Aidan and his loyal companions faced a formidable foe in the form of Pyrrhia, a sorceress with an unmatched mastery over fire. Her insidious purpose was to harness the volatile energies of the Strudderion, a realm known for its chaotic and unpredictable nature, for her dark ambitions. Pyrrhia's control over fire was beyond compare, able to conjure flames that defied the very laws of nature. Her infernos could consume everything in their path, leaving nothing but destruction. Despite the overwhelming power of their adversary, Aidan and his

45

companions stood firm in their resolve to stop Pyrrhia. The air crackled with the intensity of her fiery onslaught, and the ensuing battle was nothing short of cataclysmic. It quickly became apparent that defeating Pyrrhia would require Aidan to tap into the deepest reserves of his Nura'el abilities. Undeterred, Aidan delved deep within himself, connecting with the dormant power of the Phoenix that lay within him. Through a profound communion with the legendary bird of renewal, Aidan's being was ignited with flames of immense significance. The flames of renewal erupted from his soul, and he met Pyrrhia's fiery onslaught with his fire - a fire infused with the very essence of the fabled Phoenix itself. With the power of the Phoenix at his fingertips, Aidan was able to stand his ground against Pyrrhia's overwhelming power and emerge victorious. In a display of incredible power, Aidan emerged victorious over Pyrrhia, whose fiery abilities were no match for the elemental forces he wielded. The Phoenix's magic, which Aidan had just unlocked, proved to be the decisive factor that quenched Pyrrhia's evil ambitions. The victory not only marked the defeat of a formidable foe but also signalled Aidan's more profound connection to the Phoenix's magic. This newfound connection would play a crucial role in the cosmic battles ahead. The Strudderion, once a realm of chaos and adversity, now bore witness to Aidan's mastery over the Phoenix's fire. This momentous achievement was pivotal in Aidan's journey as a Nura'el.

Aidan and his steadfast companions reached the Stormspire Peaks after a challenging journey. This area is known for its severe weather conditions, with strong winds and harsh storms prevailing. While travelling through this dangerous terrain, they encountered a group of stormcallers who aimed to manipulate the stormy skies for unknown reasons. The leader of these stormcallers was none other than Tempestia, a sorceress of unparalleled skill who commanded the very elements of nature. With her uncanny ability to summon lightning that streaked across the heavens with blinding brilliance, conjure tornadoes that ravaged the land like voracious beasts, and command the winds to dance to her will, Tempestia was a force to be reckoned with. The ensuing battle against Tempestia and her formidable stormcallers was a fierce clash of elemental forces on an epic scale. Lightning arced across the sky in dazzling patterns, and the thunderous roars of the storm seemed to challenge the very fabric of existence. It was a trial that tested the limits of Aidan and his unwavering companions' abilities, pushing them to their core and testing the unyielding strength of their unity and resolve. Once again, Aidan delved into the depths of his Nura'el abilities. Amidst the storm's chaos, he reached out to the tempest, forging a connection with the elemental forces of air and electricity that raged around him. Lightning surged through his veins, and the winds became an extension of his will. With a burst of electrifying power, Aidan harnessed the very essence of the storm. Bolts of lightning lashed out, guided by his command, striking down Tempestia and her stormcallers in blinding flashes of brilliance. The tempest, once a relentless force of destruction, was quelled, and the skies above the Stormspire Peaks cleared. Following the tremendous battle, Aidan was enveloped by a serene tranquillity that replaced the tumultuous chaos. It was a moment of profound realisation for him as he experienced an exhilarating sensation of power that surpassed his mere control over the elements. Aidan had emerged victorious over the tempest and had become one with the essence of the skies, embodying the unbridled force of the heavens themselves. The Stormspire Peaks bore witness to Aidan's rise to prominence, a testament to his unyielding determination and the limitless potential of his Nura'el abilities. The sheer magnitude of the moment was indescribable, and Aidan knew that the experience had forever changed him.

The hardest part was yet to come as they faced the dangerous Abyssal Depths. It was a dark and risky place where they would confront the Abyssal Cult, a group of evil sorcerers with a harmful plan to bring endless darkness and hopelessness to the world. The individual who held the position of leader within the Abyssal Cult, known as Abyssalon, was a mysterious figure with a profound mastery over the art of shadow magic. This particular type of magic was believed to have originated from the deepest, darkest depths of the Abyssal Depths itself. Abyssalon's abilities in this area were unparalleled, as he could conjure shadows that could consume any light in the surrounding area. Additionally, he was able to weave intricate illusions that were capable of distorting reality itself, and he was even able to command the very essence of darkness.

Despite the inherent malevolence of his powers, Abyssalon appeared to take great pleasure in the depths of despair that he sought to create.

The battle against Abyssalon and his devoted cult was a harrowing descent into the abyss of despair. Shadows cloaked everything, and the treacherous waters of the Abyssal Depths seemed to conspire against them. It was a trial that tested their formidable abilities and the limits of their sanity. Aidan stood unwaveringly in the face of the relentless onslaught of shadows and illusions. He delved deep into the wellspring of his Nura'el abilities with a determination that burned just as brightly as the Phoenix within him. Summoning the radiant light that pierced the suffocating darkness, he fought back against the Abyssalon and his devoted followers. With powerful radiance, Aidan cast out the shadows that clung to reality and shattered the insidious illusions of Abyssalon. The evil leader of the cult was defeated, and his dark ambitions were extinguished like a waning ember in the void. Aidan emerged victorious over a formidable adversary, harnessing the purest essence of the Phoenix's magic. This light burned undiminished, even in the deepest abyss of despair. Aidan's triumph in the Abyssal Depths was a testament to his indomitable will and unbreakable connection to the Phoenix's radiant magic. His victory not only dispelled the darkness of the Abyssal Cult but also illuminated the boundless potential of the Nura'el within him.

Throughout their perilous journey, Aidan's growth as a Nura'el had been nothing short of extraordinary. With each trial and challenge they had faced, his powers had blossomed, and he had tapped into ever-deeper reserves of his Nura'el abilities. The essence of the legendary Phoenix now burned within him with an enthusiasm that rivalled the most scorching infernos, a power that transcended the elemental forces themselves. Through his unwavering determination and perseverance, Aidan had emerged victorious over formidable adversaries and treacherous trials. In doing so, he had forged an unbreakable connection to the Phoenix Stone - a cosmic artefact of immeasurable significance - whose presence seemed to pulsate with renewed vigour in his company. No longer was it a mere conduit for the Phoenix's magic; it had become an integral part of him, a tangible symbol of his cosmic purpose. As word of Aidan's exploits spread throughout the land, he became a beacon of hope and inspiration to all those who longed for a brighter future. He had become a living embodiment of the Phoenix's power, a force capable of restoring balance and igniting the flames of renewal in even the darkest times. But Aidan's journey was not one that he undertook alone. Alongside his steadfast fellowship, he had faced countless challenges and overcome seemingly insurmountable odds. He remained united in their quest to restore elemental balance and bring hope to a chaotic world.

Aidan's ascension to greatness was a testament to the indomitable spirit of the Nura'els. This legacy had been passed down through generations of warriors who had dedicated their lives to upholding the cosmic order. Though the path ahead was fraught with uncertainty, they were guided by their shared purpose, their unshakable unity, and the enduring legacy of the Nura'els. Together, they would fulfil their cosmic destiny and usher in a new era of light and renewal.

ASHES OF THE PAST

Aidan's childhood was spent in the Faelorian Forest, surrounded by ancient trees that whispered secrets to the wind and woodland creatures that danced to the rhythms of nature. Though he cherished memories of dappled sunlight and rustling leaves, thoughts of his parents were shrouded in a hazy mist, like forgotten dreams. They had passed away when he was young, and he was later raised by adoptive parents, Vilem and Elara, who taught him the ways of the forest and the importance of the Phoenix Stone. As Aidan began to fulfil his destiny as a Nura'el, he couldn't help but wonder about his origins. The mystery surrounding his parents' identity and passing lingered like a fog, and even Vilem and Elara seemed hesitant to reveal the untold chapters of his family's history. His curiosity grew stronger with each passing day, a yearning to unearth the hidden truths buried in the shadows of his past. The forest held its secrets close, whispering them only to the ancient trees and the winds that rustled through their leaves. Aidan found himself entangled in a web of questions without answers, and the more he tried to unravel the mystery of his family's legacy, the more elusive it seemed to become. As Aidan journeyed forth to fulfil the prophecy that would restore the balance to the elements, he couldn't help but be plagued by questions about his family and heritage. The legacy of the Nura'els was intricately intertwined with his identity. Still, hidden truths and mysteries remained veiled and waiting to be uncovered.

During quiet moments between his training as a Nura'el and his communion with the Phoenix Stone, Aidan often found his thoughts drifting to his parents. Who were they, and what legacy had they left behind? What cosmic forces had brought them together, and what circumstances had led to their untimely departure from his life? These were the enigmas that tugged at his soul, persistent as the ceaseless flow of the forest's streams. Yet, Aidan remained resolute in his quest for answers, for he knew that only by understanding his past could he truly fulfil his destiny as a Nura'el and restore balance to the elements. Like the dense undergrowth of the Faelorian Forest, the shrouded past concealed layers of history and significance waiting to be uncovered. Aidan understood that his journey as a Nura'el was a cosmic mission and a deeply personal quest to unravel the mysteries of his heritage. In the heart of the ancient woods, where the echoes of his parents' presence still whispered through the leaves, he stood at the threshold of a profound revelation—one that would illuminate not only the path of his destiny but also the legacy that had brought him to this pivotal moment in his life.

As Aidan and his unwavering fellowship journeyed through the vast tapestry of their quest, their path led them to an encounter that would alter the course of their journey—a meeting with an ancient oracle named Elowen. She possessed a rare and extraordinary gift that allowed her to peer into the annals of time, unveiling hidden truths that lay veiled in the cosmic tapestry. Elowen's intrigue was piqued by Aidan's profound quest, his yearning to uncover the enigmatic history of his family. It was a longing that resonated deeply with her, a shared recognition of the deep significance of one's lineage and the cosmic tapestry that bound generations together. With a benevolent smile, she extended her hand to Aidan, offering to help him unlock the mysteries of his lineage. Under the guidance of this venerable oracle, Aidan embarked on a journey of self-discovery that transcended the boundaries of time itself. With her ancient wisdom as their guiding star, they delved into the depths of Aidan's memories and the forgotten annals of his family's history. It was a voyage that would lead him to the very edges of time, granting him glimpses of the past and allowing him to witness the trials and tribulations faced by his ancestors. Through a tapestry of visions and memories, Aidan began to unravel the profound legacy woven into his very being.

His family, it appeared, had a lineage that stretched back through the ages—a lineage of Nura'els. They had stood as steadfast guardians of the Phoenix Stone for generations, and their sacred duty passed down from parent to child like a torch that illuminated the path of cosmic destiny.

In these vivid recollections of the past, Aidan saw his ancestors in their shining glory, their commitment to preserving the elemental balance and protecting the Phoenix Stone unwavering. They had been warriors and scholars, drawn together by a shared purpose and a cosmic kinship that transcended time and space. The legacy of the Nura'els coursed through his veins, a testament to the enduring strength of those who had come before him. Yet, amidst the radiant tapestry of his family's history, one story remained hidden—a tale shrouded in the mists of time, obscured by the passage of generations. It was the story of his parents, Raphael and Isolde, who had stood together as Nura'els against a formidable and relentless adversary—an enraged Phoenix corrupted by the insidious touch of dark forces. Aidan delved deeper into these memories, he witnessed the trials and tribulations faced by his parents. Their love for each other had been a beacon of hope in the face of adversity, a love forged in the crucible of cosmic battles and tested by the very forces of darkness they sought to quell. They had been partners in life and destiny, their spirits intertwined like the eternal dance of fire and air.

The corrupted Phoenix, a once-majestic guardian of renewal, had succumbed to the insidious tendrils of darkness, becoming an instrument of chaos and destruction. Once resplendent with cosmic light, its feathers were now tainted with the shadowy essence that had trapped it. With every beat of its fiery wings, it unleashed an unholy fury upon the world, scorching the land it had once nurtured. The havoc wrought by the corrupted Phoenix knew no bounds. Villages and towns were reduced to smouldering ruins, their inhabitants fleeing in terror from the all-consuming inferno. The world, which had thrived under the watchful gaze of the Phoenix, now cowered in the face of its wrath, the elemental balance hanging in a precarious balance. Amidst this tumultuous chaos, a glimmer of hope emerged—a hope forged in the hearts of two remarkable individuals, Raphael and Isolde, Aidan's parents. They were not merely guardians of the Phoenix Stone; they were warriors of unparalleled skill and unyielding courage. Together, they had risen to the daunting challenge that threatened to plunge the world into eternal darkness. Their love for their son, Aidan, and unwavering duty to protect the world fuelled their resolve.

The battle against the corrupted Phoenix had been monumental and arduous, a cosmic struggle that threatened to shatter the very foundations of their world. The skies became a canvas of fiery chaos as the Phoenix unleashed wrath upon them. The very heavens trembled at the fury of its elemental onslaught. The elemental balance had hung in the balance, and the fate of their realm teetered on the precipice of chaos. Raphael and Isolde had stood resolute, drawing upon the Phoenix's magic and the legacy of their ancestors to confront the evil adversary. In a blaze of elemental fury and unwavering determination, they had engaged in a cosmic battle that transcended the ordinary. Their powers intertwined like cosmic threads, weaving a tapestry of elemental might and unwavering determination. In a blaze of radiant fury, they confronted the corrupted Phoenix, their hearts ablaze with love for each other and an uncompromising duty to restore the elemental balance. The battle that ensued was a spectacle of cosmic forces, the clashing of elemental energies that shook the very foundations of the world. Fire and light met shadow and darkness in a dance of elemental fury, each force vying for supremacy. The skies roared with thunderous applause, and the earth quaked beneath the weight of their struggle. As the battle raged, Raphael and Isolde's love and determination proved their greatest weapons. They channelled the essence of the Nura'el with an unparalleled unity, their powers combining in a blinding crescendo of elemental might. Together, they managed to weaken the corrupted Phoenix, their cosmic efforts stripping it of the evil influence that had ensnared its essence. In a radiant eruption of elemental forces, the corrupted Phoenix's shadowy shackles were shattered and freed from the clutches of darkness that had trapped it. The once-majestic guardian of renewal was restored to its true cosmic essence, a being of light and rebirth once more. But victory came at a profound cost. In its evil fury, the corrupted Phoenix had one final, desperate gambit—an explosion of fire and chaos that bore the potential to consume everything in its infernal embrace. The very fabric of reality quaked at the impending cataclysm, and it was in this dire moment that Raphael and Isolde, bound by love and duty, made a heart-wrenching decision. With a heavy heart, they turned their unwavering determination toward a fateful act of sacrifice that would resonate through the annals of time as a testament to the boundless love and courage of the Nura'els. In a cosmic display of unity and selflessness, they summoned their combined powers, intertwining their essences like two stars in the celestial firmament.

Their actions were driven by a profound understanding of the peril that enveloped their world and their responsibility as protectors of the Phoenix Stone. They knew their son's survival, Aidan, was intertwined with the world's salvation. In a moment of sublime clarity, they made the ultimate sacrifice that would leave an indelible mark on the tapestry of cosmic destiny. The air seemed to tremble as the enigmatic forces clashed with titanic intensity, a battle that threatened to reshape the world's destiny. As the corrupted Phoenix's cataclysmic explosion of fire and chaos surged, Raphael and Isolde's unified power formed a radiant barrier—a shield of love and sacrifice that encased their young son, Aidan, in its protective embrace. The inferno raged around them, its searing heat and blinding light a testament to the cosmic struggle that had taken place. But within the protective cocoon of their sacrifice, Aidan was untouched by the consuming flames. His parents' love and courage had shielded him from the fiery maelstrom that sought to engulf the world. In that moment of heart-rending sacrifice, the legacy of the Nura'els reached its zenith. This gift transcended the elemental balance and resonated with the heart of the cosmos. The battle had exacted a toll on Raphael and Isolde that could not be reversed. Their bodies bore the scars of their cosmic struggle, their spirits forever marked by their trials. Their son, Aidan, entrusted with the profound duty of a Nura'el, would carry the legacy of their heroic sacrifice. As the echoes of their battle reverberated through time and space, Raphael and Isolde's love and sacrifice remained etched in the cosmic tapestry. They had been protectors of the Phoenix Stone and beacons of hope and courage in the face of overwhelming darkness. Their legacy was a testament to the enduring power of love, duty, and cosmic destiny. This legacy would illuminate the path of Aidan's journey as a Nura'el, guiding him through the trials and tribulations yet to come. The culmination of the cosmic battle between Raphael, Isolde, and the corrupted Phoenix reached its zenith in a cataclysmic moment of reckoning. The cataclysmic explosion unleashed by the corrupted Phoenix had repercussions that reverberated through time and space. The world was spared from the impending doom, its elemental balance preserved by the selfless act of two courageous souls. Yet, Raphael and Isolde, the valiant Nura'els, paid the ultimate price for their heroism.

In the aftermath of the cataclysm, their presence in the physical realm was no more. They had become cosmic spirits, their essences interwoven with the very fabric of the Phoenix Stone. This sacred artefact held the heart of the Phoenix's magic and the legacy of countless generations of protectors. The Phoenix Stone pulsed with renewed strength, its radiance a testament to the indomitable spirit of the Nura'els and the love that had guided their actions. The legacy of Raphael and Isolde, Aidan's parents, remained alive in the Phoenix Stone—a radiant reminder of their love, sacrifice, and unwavering commitment to the cosmic order. Though known to few, their story was etched into the heart of the world, a narrative thread that connected the past, present, and future. Aidan stood before the Phoenix Stone, and his parents' sacrifice weighed heavy on his heart. The burden of their legacy and the responsibility of a Nura'el now rested squarely upon his shoulders. He had been spared by their sacrifice, chosen to carry forward the cosmic mission that had been their life's work. During his grief and reverence for his parents, Aidan found strength. Their love and sacrifice had illuminated the path of his destiny. This approach would require unwavering determination and harnessing the Phoenix's magic within him. Their legacy, pulsing within the Phoenix Stone, served as a guiding light—a reminder that the bonds of family, duty, and love transcended the boundaries of time and space.

With renewed purpose, Aidan vowed to honour the legacy of Raphael and Isolde, the Nura'els who had sacrificed everything for the world's renewal. Though shrouded in the mists of time, their story would live on through him—a legacy of love, sacrifice, and cosmic destiny that would guide him through the trials and tribulations of his journey as a Nura'el. The revelation of his parents' sacrifice and their heroic battle against the corrupted Phoenix marked a pivotal moment in Aidan's journey. This moment transcended duty and touched the very core of his being. In the wake of this profound revelation, Aidan found himself bound not only by the chains of responsibility but by the threads of destiny itself. His journey as a Nura'el had transformed from a mere duty into a cosmic mandate, a legacy that pulsed through his veins with each beat of his heart. The echoes of his parents' sacrifice reverberated within him. This sacred artefact held the essence of the Phoenix's magic and the legacy of countless generations of protectors. Here, in the heart of the Faelorian Forest, Aidan felt the profound weight of his heritage and the enduring spirit of his family's legacy. The revelation of his family's history and their role as Nura'els unveiled a tapestry of cosmic destiny that had long been mysterious. No longer was Aidan merely fulfilling a duty passed down through the ages; he was embracing a destiny that had chosen him, a destiny intertwined with the very essence of the Phoenix itself. Aidan's connection to the Phoenix's magic grew more robust with each challenge and foe they confronted. He could feel the presence of his parents, Raphael and Isolde, guiding him from the cosmic realms where their spirits now resided. Their essence, bound to the Phoenix Stone, had become a part of him—a guiding light that illuminated his path as he walked in their footsteps. The legacy of the Nura'els was not a mere historical footnote; it was a living, breathing force that coursed through Aidan's being. The trials and tribulations of his family's lineage had not been in vain; they had forged a legacy of courage, sacrifice, and unwavering determination. Each generation of Nura'els had faced the darkness and adversity that threatened the world, and each had emerged victorious, rekindling hope and renewal in the wake of cosmic turmoil.

With newfound clarity and purpose, Aidan understood that he carried not only the legacy of his ancestors but also the profound love and sacrifice of his parents. Their story, long forgotten by the world, had been etched into the cosmic tapestry, a narrative thread that would guide him in the trials yet to come. As he gazed upon the radiant Phoenix Stone, he knew that his quest was not only a mission to restore the elemental balance but also a tribute to the enduring legacy of the Nura'els who had come before him—a legacy that pulsed within his very heart, a fire of determination and renewal that would illuminate the path of his cosmic destiny. The tapestry of this epic tale unfurled against a backdrop of unprecedented calamity—a time when the elemental balance of the world hung by a thread, teetering on the precipice of annihilation. It was an era when the very foundations of the earth trembled, and the Phoenix Stone's magic, once a beacon of renewal and cosmic harmony, had waned to a feeble flicker. In this dire hour, an evil force had seized control of the legendary Phoenix—a being that had long been a symbol of hope and rebirth. As Aidan continued his journey, he did so with a renewed sense of purpose and an understanding that he was not alone in his quest. Though physically absent, his parents were with him in spirit, their presence a constant source of guidance and inspiration. They had become part of the living legacy of the Nura'els, a lineage that transcended time and space. The bond between Aidan and his family's legacy was not one of duty alone but a profound connection that ran deeper than blood. He was not merely a Nura'el by destiny; he was a Nura'el by birthright. His family's legacy, a tapestry woven with threads of courage, love, and sacrifice, now burned within him like a sacred flame. With every challenge they faced, Aidan drew strength from the knowledge that he was carrying forward a legacy that had faced darkness and adversity time and again, emerging victorious with the Phoenix's magic as their ally. He was a guardian of the elemental balance and a steward of his family's heritage. This heritage bore the weight of countless generations dedicated to protecting the world from cosmic threats. The veil of ancestry had been lifted, revealing a duty and a cosmic destiny that bound him to the very essence of the Phoenix. His journey was no longer a solitary quest but a testament to the enduring power of family, heritage, and the unbreakable bonds that connected him to the Phoenix's magic.

The legacy of his family's courage and sacrifice became a source of inspiration for all who stood by his side. They had witnessed the unveiling of his destiny and the cosmic connection that bound him to the Phoenix Stone and the Phoenix's magic. It was a lineage that had faced adversity and emerged triumphant, a family symbolising the enduring power of renewal and hope. The challenges ahead were daunting, but Aidan faced them with the knowledge that he carried the legacy of the Nura'els and the enduring spirit of his family. He was a Nura'el, not only by the decree of destiny but by the very blood that flowed through his veins. The legacy of his family's courage, sacrifice, and cosmic destiny burned within him like a sacred torch. It illuminated the path to renewal and hope in a world yearning for cosmic balance.

CELESTIAL ENCOUNTER

An enchanted forest surrounded Aidan and his steadfast companions as they made camp near the tranquil waters of the Celestial Lake. The campfire crackled softly, casting fleeting shadows upon the nearby trees and illuminating the serene surroundings. The air was still as if nature was preparing for an event of cosmic importance. In this calm moment of reprieve, amidst the whispers of the night and the gentle rustling of leaves, the celestial encounter unfolded—a celestial encounter that would forever alter the course of Aidan's destiny. In the midst of their arduous journey, Aidan and his fellowship found themselves standing at a critical moment that would test their fortitude and reshape their understanding of their cosmic connection to the Phoenix Stone and the Phoenix—the moment had been orchestrated by a celestial being whose presence held the key to a revelation of immense significance. From the heavens above, where stars glimmered like precious gems and constellations told stories of forgotten epochs, descended a figure of shining radiance.

Mikha'el, the celestial being, descended upon the mortal realm with an aura of unparalleled luminosity. His wings, majestic and expansive as the breadth of the night sky, stretched forth in celestial grace. Clad in armour that seemed woven from the very fabric of the cosmos, it shimmered with an otherworldly lustre akin to the brilliance of distant stars. Mikha'el's arrival was not merely a physical presence but a celestial event—a convergence of mortal and divine realms. His ethereal presence cast a radiant glow that bathed the campsite in a warm, golden embrace as if the very

59

essence of starlight had chosen this sacred moment to descend upon the earth. Mikha'el alighted before Aidan and his companions, his luminous visage held the wisdom of ages. This ancient and eternal understanding transcended the boundaries of time and mortality. His eyes, like pools of celestial knowledge, gazed upon them with a depth that hinted at the secrets of the cosmos. The arrival of Mikha'el was a moment that Aidan and his companions would never forget, as it marked a turning point in their journey and a revelation of cosmic significance that would alter the course of their lives forever.

Greetings, Nura'el," Mikha'el's celestial voice echoed with a resonance that evoked a harmonious melody, not just in the ears but in the souls of those who heard it. He had descended from the celestial realms to guide Aidan on the path he treads, which was entwined with destiny, bound by the cosmic threads of the Phoenix Stone and the Phoenix. Mikha'el's words were imbued with an ethereal weight that hung like a celestial proclamation. His presence, words, and radiant aura were awe-inspiring. In this moment, the mortal and the divine stood at the threshold of an extraordinary revelation. Mikha'el's words would unravel the mysteries of Aidan's connection to the Phoenix Stone and the legendary Phoenix. Mikha'el, the celestial being, stood before Aidan and his companions, radiating a luminous presence illuminating the path ahead. His words were unveiling a cosmic truth that transcended the boundaries of mortal comprehension. Mikha'el began to speak, the atmosphere around the campfire seemed to still further, and Aidan and his companions listened with profound and almost reverent attention. At that moment, the boundaries between the earthly and divine blurred, and Mikha'el unravelled a revelation that transcended the comprehension of mere mortals. The revelation unveiled the true nature of the Phoenix and the Phoenix Stone, and it was a testament to the grandeur of the cosmos. Mikha'el's voice resonated like a cosmic symphony. He revealed that long ago when the cosmos was but a tapestry in the loom of existence, the Phoenix held a role far grander than that of a mere symbol of renewal. It was a celestial guardian, a cosmic sentinel entrusted with the weighty task of bridging the realms between life and death, creation and dissolution.

The Phoenix Stone, an artefact that Aidan now protects with unwavering devotion, is not just a relic; it is a fragment of the cosmic flame itself, a luminous beacon that sustains the intricate cycles of the universe. Mikha'el's words, pregnant with profound cosmic truths, began to unfurl before Aidan and his companions, an indescribable sensation coursed through their very beings. It was as if the threads of destiny were being woven before their eyes, which connected them to the vast tapestry of the universe itself. The Phoenix, once perceived as a magnificent bird of fire, now emerged as a celestial entity, an embodiment of cosmic purpose and order. Aidan listened to Mikha'el's revelation, he felt an inexplicable resonance deep within his soul. It was as if his heart, like the Phoenix Stone itself, was pulsating in unison with the cosmic forces that governed the universe. The significance of his role as a Nura'el was no longer limited to mortal duties. Still, it had become an integral part of the grand cosmic narrative that spanned across dimensions, epochs, and the essence of creation itself. The realisation that the Phoenix Stone was not just a mere artefact but a fragment of the cosmic flame, a vital element that served to maintain the delicate equilibrium of the universe, was a profound revelation for Aidan. Mikha'el's words illuminated the cosmic nature of their quest and placed a responsibility that reached far beyond the boundaries of their mortal lives upon their shoulders.

It filled him with an overwhelming sense of awe and reverence, and he understood that his duty as a Nura'el was not an isolated task but an interconnected thread in the cosmic tapestry. The Phoenix Stone, a radiant beacon in the tapestry of existence, played a vital role in sustaining the cycles of creation and dissolution, a crucial nexus point where cosmic forces converged. It blurred the boundaries between life and death and served as a dwelling place for the essence of the Phoenix's magic. The Phoenix, in its truest form, was a guardian of the cosmic order, standing as a sentinel at the threshold of existence itself. Realising that his journey as a Nura'el was not just a personal quest but a cosmic duty filled Aidan with a sense of purpose that surpassed mortal comprehension. He understood that he was not only a protector of an artefact but a steward of the cosmic flame, a beacon of hope and renewal in a universe on the brink of chaos. As the campfire flickered, its flames echoing the cosmic love itself, Aidan realised that the night sky, with its myriad of stars, now bore witness to the unfolding cosmic narrative. His bond with Mikha'el, his celestial guide, and the divine forces that governed the cosmos had been forged in the crucible of heavenly revelation. The journey ahead was not easy, but he knew that he was now part of something much more significant than himself. This narrative transcended time and space.

The revelation had transformed their quest into a pilgrimage of cosmic significance, a voyage into the heart of creation itself. Aidan contemplated the profound responsibility entrusted to him, he felt a sense of duty and obligation that extended far beyond his role as a guardian. The Phoenix Stone, once a treasured artefact, had become a cosmic nexus, an anchor that held the universe in delicate balance. Aidan's role as a Nura'el was not merely that of a protector but that of a cosmic steward entrusted with preserving the equilibrium of existence. The encounter with Mikha'el had bound Aidan and his companions to a cosmic destiny that resonated not only through the annals of history but across the tapestry of the universe itself. With newfound clarity and purpose, they prepared to embark on a journey that would determine the destiny of not just their world but the entirety of creation.

Mikha'el's ethereal presence remained a beacon in the stillness of the night, shining in celestial radiance. His wings, expansive as the night sky, seemed to cradle the cosmos. In the wake of his profound revelation about the cosmic nature of the Phoenix and the Phoenix Stone, Mikha'el's words carried a gravity far beyond the earthly realm.

Aidan stood at a crossroads, a decision determining the fate of existence itself. He had to choose whether to embrace his role as a guardian of the cosmic flame, protecting the Phoenix Stone for his world and the delicate balance that sustained the universe. Alternatively, he could turn away from this profound responsibility,

allowing the cosmic equilibrium to falter. As Mikha'el spoke, there was a palpable shift in the air, as if the very fabric of reality quivered under the weight of the decision that now hung in the balance. The campfire, its flames dancing in harmonious response to the cosmic revelation, flickered with newfound intensity. The starlit canopy above bore witness to a moment of cosmic significance, where the fate of existence itself hung in the balance. For Aidan, the words of the celestial being reverberated within the depths of his being. The choice he now faced was not a mere decision but a cosmic responsibility that transcended the boundaries of mortal understanding. It was a choice that carried with it the destiny of not just his world but the entirety of creation. It was an unfathomable responsibility that stretched across the reaches of the universe. In that profound moment, he understood that this decision was not his alone to make. It was a collective choice involving his fellowship and all future generations of Nura'els. Their destinies, their actions, and the legacy they would leave behind were inexorably linked to this pivotal decision. Aidan contemplated the gravity of the choice before him, his gaze shifted to his companions, who sat in respectful silence, their faces

illuminated by the celestial glow of Mikha'el's presence. Lirael, with her unwavering loyalty and mastery over water; Nalorin, the guardian of the earth with roots that ran as deep as the mountains; Kaelen, whose mastery over the winds whispered of boundless potential, and Ophelia, the ancient forest spirit whose wisdom transcended the ages—all of them bore witness to this moment of cosmic import.

They were the Phoenix Stone stewards, the cosmic flame guardians, and the protectors of the universe's delicate balance. Aidan was filled with a profound sense of humility as he realised that his actions, choices, and unity with his fellowship would shape the destiny of creation itself. Their journey was not just a quest for personal glory or the fulfilment of a prophecy but a sacred duty that bound them to the very fabric of existence. As they sat by the campfire, Mikha'el, with his wings outstretched in a celestial display, gazed upon Aidan and his companions with serene wisdom. He emphasised the magnitude of their choice - to embrace the weighty responsibility of cosmic guardianship or to turn away from it. The destiny of the Phoenix Stone and the Phoenix, intertwined with the fate of the cosmos, now rested in the hands of mortals. The fellowship exchanged glances, conveying a shared understanding of the monumental path ahead. At this moment, Aidan and his companions stood at the crossroads of cosmic responsibility. Their choice would determine the course of their journey and the universe's destiny. Mikha'el's celestial revelation had expanded their perception of their quest, revealing it as more than a mere earthly undertaking. Their journey was now a cosmic endeavour intricately woven into the grand tapestry of creation itself. They were no longer just guardians of a relic; they were cosmic stewards entrusted with preserving the cosmic order. Aidan and his companions felt a profound shift within themselves as the luminescent aura of Mikha'el's presence gradually faded into the boundless expanse of the night sky. Their quest was no longer about renewing their world but safeguarding the universe's equilibrium.

The task before them was a complex one. It was a cosmic odyssey, a sacred pilgrimage to preserve the cosmic order. Each of them had been chosen for their unique abilities and strengths, and their journey had taken them through trials and tribulations that had forged unbreakable bonds between them. Now, those bonds took on a more profound significance, binding them to each other and the very cosmos itself. Aidan looked into the eyes of his companions, he saw the reflection of his determination mirrored in their gazes. They had come so far together, and their journey had evolved into something much more significant than they had ever anticipated. It was a journey that would require unwavering dedication and sacrifice, for the universe's fate hung in the balance.

In the silence that followed, the fellowship made an unspoken vow. A vow to embrace their cosmic responsibilities with unwavering dedication, to protect the Phoenix Stone for their world and the delicate balance that sustained the universe's eternal dance. They knew that their quest was not a mortal endeavour. It was a cosmic calling to shape the destiny of creation itself.

Their campfire, now a symbol of cosmic unity, blazed with an inner light that seemed to echo the radiance of the Phoenix Stone itself. As they ventured into the night, they carried with them the profound understanding that their quest was not just a journey but a sacred duty that demanded the utmost respect and devotion. Each step they took was a step towards upholding the universe's balance and illuminating the cosmic darkness with the fires of renewal and hope.

THE COSMIC CONFRONTATION

Aidan's journey came to another epic confrontation that would have far-reaching consequences. The battle was not only for the Phoenix Stone but for the universe's balance.

The night was oppressively dark, with an ominous aura that hung heavily over the land. Moldark, an evil figure of darkness, cast his shadow upon the earth, his presence sending shivers through the heavens themselves. Even the moon, usually tranquil and radiant, took on a foreboding crimson hue as if warning of the impending danger. Moldark's army, clad in armour as dark as the abyss and wielding magic tainted by their newfound allegiance to their master, descended upon the world. They marched forward with a chilling determination, exuding a profound malevolence that threatened to consume all in their path. These soldiers were not just ordinary warriors; they were once the staunchest guardians of cosmic order, tasked with safeguarding the delicate balance of the universe. However, now twisted by Moldark's insidious influence, they had become instruments of chaos, and their once-honourable duty had been perverted into a relentless quest for power and dominion. Their arrival was a portentous harbinger of impending turmoil and strife. As they advanced, the earth seemed to tremble beneath their feet, unable to bear the weight of their corrupt intentions. Their march echoed with a sense of duty distorted by malice, and it was evident that they were willing to do whatever it took to achieve their master's sinister goals. Moldark's ambition knew no bounds, and his insatiable desire to disrupt the delicate equilibrium of the universe sent shivers through the cosmos itself. The Phoenix

Stone, a symbol of renewal and cosmic harmony, was the coveted prize at the centre of his dark designs. In his obsession, he sought to wrench it from its sacred pedestal and bend its cosmic power to his evil will.

The world, once a realm of balance and serenity, now stood on the precipice of an abyss. Moldark's looming shadow threatened to cast creation into eternal turmoil, extinguishing the cosmic flame of hope and ushering in an era of unending darkness. The universe's fate hung in the balance as his forces marched closer to their nefarious goal. The world trembled in anticipation of the cataclysmic confrontation on the horizon, and the stakes had never been higher. The stage for the impending confrontation was none other than the hallowed ground of the Cosmic Nexus—a place of profound significance in the intricate tapestry of the cosmos itself. It was a realm of ethereal beauty and cosmic significance, was witness to a convergence of celestial energies and cosmic phenomena that defied mortal comprehension. It was a place where the cosmic dance of creation and dissolution unfolded in perpetuity, and the boundaries between dimensions were malleable. The interplay of cosmic forces was both mesmerising and dangerous, with the destiny of galaxies and star systems converging in this liminal space. Here, at the epicentre of celestial forces, the boundaries between dimensions were rendered fragile, like gossamer threads awaiting a gentle breeze. The very fabric of existence seemed to quiver with anticipation, aware that it stood on the precipice of a cosmic clash that would reverberate through the annals of time. The Nexus was a breathtaking sight, with iridescent nebulae and constellations adorned the cosmic canvas with hues of indigo and violet. From supernovae to cosmic storms, Celestial phenomena punctuated the cosmic backdrop, lending an otherworldly grandeur to the arena of impending conflict. Moreover, a sense of profound anticipation permeated the air, an anticipation that transcended mere mortal understanding. Each cosmic entity and celestial body seemed to hold its breath, poised in a state of heightened awareness. The balance of the cosmos, a delicate equilibrium that had endured through aeons, now hung in the balance, and the foundations of existence quivered in response.

Beneath the veneer of cosmic splendour, an underlying tension was palpable, an awareness that the impending clash would shape the destiny of worlds and the cosmic order itself. It resonated through the very foundations of the Nexus, and the forces of light and darkness were on the brink of a collision, echoing through the celestial realms. In this sacred realm where the cosmos converged, the impending cosmic battle would leave an indelible mark on the eternal tapestry of creation. The universe was a silent witness, aware that the outcome would determine the fate of the Phoenix Stone and the very fabric of existence. In this awe-inspiring cosmic arena, Aidan and his steadfast fellowship stood as a living testament to the power of unity. This unity transcended the mortal realm and resonated with the very essence of the universe itself. No longer were they mere mortals embarking on a quest; they had ascended to the status of celestial champions, defenders of the cosmic order. The legacy of the Nura'els passed down through generations is coursed through their veins, and the Phoenix Stone's radiant energy pulsed within them. This eternal flame burned with unwavering resolve. The fellowship, comprised of individuals whose destinies had intertwined with the Phoenix Stone and the Phoenix's magic, now stood shoulder to shoulder on the cosmic stage. Each member possessed unique abilities and strengths, honed through trials and forged in adversity. Together, they were a formidable force, a collective embodiment of hope and determination that defied the encroaching darkness.

Ophelia, the wise and ancient forest spirit who had guided Aidan since his formative years, stood at the forefront of this celestial assembly. Her presence was a radiant beacon amidst the looming shadows, a living embodiment of the Phoenix Stone's wisdom and the cumulative knowledge of generations. Her eyes held the ageless wisdom of epochs long past, and her voice, when she spoke, resonated through the celestial expanse like the harmonious chords of the cosmos itself. With a voice that carried the authority of aeons, Ophelia addressed the fellowship, her words echoing through the cosmic arena and resonating profoundly.

"United we stand," she proclaimed, her words imbued with the weight of cosmic significance, "for we are not just protectors of the

Phoenix Stone; we are stewards of the cosmic order itself. Together, we shall defend the Phoenix Stone, preserving its sacred essence and the delicate equilibrium that sustains the universe."

Her words were a declaration and a profound affirmation of their cosmic responsibility. They were guardians of more than just a sacred artefact; they were entrusted with the fate of creation itself. The Phoenix Stone, a fragment of the cosmic flame that sustained the universe's cycles, was both a symbol and a vessel of immense cosmic power. Its significance transcended the boundaries of their world, extending to the very fabric of the cosmos. The fellowship, their hearts ablaze with purpose, nodded in solemn agreement. They understood that their quest had evolved into something far greater than they had initially imagined. It was no longer a mere mortal endeavour but a cosmic mission—a mission to safeguard the Phoenix Stone and, in doing so, preserve the balance of the universe. Their strengths and abilities converged as they stood united on the cosmic battlefield, forming a tapestry of cosmic energy that pulsed with radiant determination. It was a unity born of shared destiny and a deep and unwavering bond forged through trials and tribulations. The power of unity, they realised, was their greatest weapon. This force could rival even the darkest of cosmic adversaries. In this pivotal moment, surrounded by the celestial wonders of the Nexus, they embraced their role as heavenly champions, ready to confront the looming darkness and protect the Phoenix Stone with every fibre of their being. The fellowship's collective resolve reverberated through the cosmic expanse, a declaration to the universe that they would stand undaunted in the face of adversity. The cosmos, bearing witness to their unwavering determination, seemed to respond with a subtle shift—a realignment of stars and celestial energies that signalled the universe's acknowledgement of their purpose. As they prepared to confront the forces of darkness that loomed on the horizon, the fellowship's unity remained unbreakable, spirits intertwined with the very fabric of existence. The cosmic stage was set, and the destiny of worlds hung in the balance as they readied themselves for the cosmic battle that would determine the fate of the Phoenix Stone and the cosmic order itself. The Cosmic Nexus quivered with anticipation as the cosmic clash between light and darkness unfurled in an eruption of cataclysmic fury.

Moldark, the embodiment of malevolence, strode forward at the forefront of his shadowy army. His presence consumed the surrounding light, casting an ominous pall over the celestial battleground. As he advanced, the moon, which had once bathed the Nexus in silvery radiance, shifted to a blood-red hue as if recoiling in fear from the impending darkness. Moldark's eyes blazed with an unholy fire, their depths concealing aeons of twisted ambitions. His outstretched hand crackled with dark energies, an ominous aura that threatened to unravel the very threads of creation. His footsteps echoed through the cosmic arena, each resonating with the foreboding weight of his evil intent. Facing him, Aidan stood as a beacon of unwavering resolve. His journey had led him to this moment, where he confronted not only a physical adversary but the embodiment of cosmic disruption. The revelation of the Phoenix Stone's true significance, unveiled by Mikha'el, had fortified his spirit and deepened his understanding of the delicate balance that governed the universe.

The duel between Aidan and Moldark was nothing short of a spectacle of cosmic might. Aidan's Nura'el abilities, now honed by his awareness of the universe's intricate web, clashed with the evil sorcery that emanated from his adversary. Their every movement sent shockwaves rippling through the very fabric of the Cosmic Nexus, distorting the boundaries between reality and the astral. Aidan's eyes blazed with a determined fire as he channelled the essence of the Phoenix's magic that burned within him. Not just power surged through his veins, but an understanding—a profound connection to the cosmic forces that governed creation and dissolution. Each strike of his blade, each surge of elemental energy, resonated with the harmony of the cosmos. Moldark, fueled by the darkest of intentions, countered with spells that twisted the laws of reality. Shadows congealed into ethereal blades that lashed out with an evil hunger, seeking to extinguish Aidan's light. Dark tendrils of magic, like serpents of cosmic discord, slithered through the Nexus, threatening to trap all in their path.

The clash between their opposing forces sent shockwaves of cosmic energy reverberating through the Nexus. Stars shimmered and danced in response to the celestial battle, bearing witness to a conflict that transcended the boundaries of mere mortals.

Amid this cosmic duel, the members of Aidan's fellowship faced their formidable adversaries. Lirael, the master of water, engaged in a breathtaking battle with a shadowy figure who wielded the powers of frost and darkness. Their elemental strikes created crystalline explosions and obsidian shards that filled the air with an ethereal symphony of light and shadow. Kaelen, whose affinity lay with the forces of air, was locked in a tempestuous confrontation with a foe who commanded the very winds themselves. Lightning arced across the cosmic expanse, and tornadoes of celestial energy whirled around them as they grappled with elemental might. Nalorin, the guardian of earth, faced a formidable adversary whose mastery over the ground beneath them created seismic upheavals and titanic clashes. Mountains of cosmic energy rose and fell as they clashed in a contest for elemental dominance. And at the heart of the cosmic vortex stood Ophelia, the luminescent forest spirit, her presence a radiant beacon amidst the encroaching shadows. She engaged in a battle of pure essence, confronting the shadowy lieutenants of Moldark with an aura of purity and light that defied the evil forces they wielded. Ophelia's radiant and harmonious magic dispelled the malevolent incantations of her adversaries with a grace that spoke of millennia of wisdom. Her every gesture seemed to resonate with the cosmic forces beneath the surface of their battle, revealing the profound connection between the Phoenix Stone and the essence of creation.

As the clash of powers unfolded on the celestial battlefield, the Cosmic Nexus seemed to hold its breath, caught in a cosmic struggle that defied mortal comprehension. The luminous stars adorned the cosmic tapestry shimmered with intensity, their light refracted by the titanic clashes of elemental and shadowy forces.

During the battle, Aidan's connection to the Phoenix Stone deepened further. The radiant energy of the artefact pulsed within him, aligning his every action with the cosmic harmony that governed the universe. He channelled the essence of the Phoenix's magic, summoning flames of renewal that erupted in blazes of brilliant fire. The cosmic clash raged on, a testament to the unyielding determination of Aidan and his fellowship. Each member, bound by destiny and united in purpose, channelled their elemental powers with a precision and unity that defied the evil forces arrayed against them. The cosmic arena became a canvas upon which the fate of worlds was painted in the vibrant hues of elemental mastery and celestial conflict. Amidst the chaos and the cosmic clash, the fellowship remained resolute. Their hearts beat in synchrony with the universe's rhythm, their spirits intertwined with the very essence of creation. The balance of cosmic forces hung in the balance. As stars bore witness to their celestial battle, they fought for the Phoenix Stone and the delicate equilibrium that sustained the universe itself.

Aidan found himself at the precipice of destiny, standing in a cosmic battle that threatened to disrupt the universe's balance. At the heart of this conflict was the Phoenix Stone, a powerful heavenly flame that held the essence of creation within its depths. It had been entrusted to the Nura'els for generations, and its significance was no longer confined to the mortal realm but extended to the very fabric of the cosmos. As Aidan faced Moldark, the embodiment of malice, he grew to understand the true nature of the Phoenix Stone's power. It was not merely a tool for manipulating elements or magic but a force of renewal that embodied the cosmic balance of the universe. Aidan realised that he could not allow such cosmic disruption to prevail and that the Phoenix Stone was not a weapon to be controlled by evil. It was a guardian of harmony, a force of cosmic equilibrium. With unwavering determination, Aidan embraced the Phoenix Stone's power, and its radiant energy enveloped him like a mantle of pure cosmic force. The transformation was as if the Phoenix Stone had recognised Aidan as its rightful protector. His very being resonated with the cosmic energy, and his connection to the Phoenix Stone transcended the bounds of the mortal coil. The Phoenix Stone's luminous energy flowed through him, Aidan's aura blazed with an incandescent brilliance that dispelled the encroaching darkness.

The shadows that had clung to Moldark's form began to wither and retreat, unable to withstand the overwhelming purity of the Phoenix Stone's radiance. The cosmic battlefield shook in response to this monumental shift in power. Stars above shimmered with renewed intensity as if rejoicing in the alignment of a true guardian with the Phoenix Stone. The very fabric of the universe seemed to resonate with Aidan's embodied harmony, and the celestial bodies bore witness to this transcendent moment. Moldark's malevolent intentions thwarted by the Phoenix Stone's radiant might recoil in the face of Aidan's cosmic power. The obsidian armour that had once been a symbol of his dominion over darkness cracked and crumbled, revealing a form corrupted and consumed by malignancy. Aidan, an embodiment of cosmic balance, advanced with purpose. His blade, infused with the Phoenix Stone's energy, gleamed with the brilliance of a thousand stars. He channelled the essence of the Phoenix's magic with each strike, unleashing flames that cleansed and renewed. The battle between light and darkness climaxed, and Moldark became increasingly powerless in the face of Aidan's radiant onslaught. The cosmic forces that had once answered to his malevolence now rebelled, repelled by the brilliant purity of the Phoenix Stone.

In a final, desperate gambit, Moldark summoned the remnants of his dark forces to assail Aidan. Shadows coalesced into a vortex of cosmic discord, a storm of darkness that threatened to engulf all in its path. But Aidan, now in complete harmony with the Phoenix Stone, stood unwavering. Aidan summoned the Phoenix Stone's power in its fullest glory with a resounding cry that echoed through the Cosmic Nexus. The radiant energy surged from him in a bright wave that swept away the cosmic discord, dispersing the shadows and dispelling the evil forces. Moldark, stripped of his dark powers and powerless, could only watch as the Phoenix Stone's energy enveloped him. The cosmic flame's brilliance seared away the hostility that had consumed him, leaving behind a being of purity and light. It was a transformation that mirrored the renewal the Phoenix Stone embodied.

In the wake of the cosmic upheaval, Moldark, now free from the shackles of malevolence, stood as a testament to the power of renewal and cosmic balance. The Phoenix Stone's radiance had cleansed not only Aidan's adversary but the very fabric of the universe itself. With a solemn purpose, Aidan approached Moldark, extending a hand of reconciliation. The cosmic battle had concluded, and the forces of darkness had been defeated, not through destruction but through the power of renewal and transformation. Moldark, humbled by the events that had transpired, accepted Aidan's hand. It was a moment of cosmic redemption, a symbol of the enduring potential for renewal and harmony, even in the face of malice. Once locked in a cosmic clash, the two adversaries now stood united by a shared understanding of the Phoenix Stone's true purpose. The Cosmic Nexus, a vast and awe-inspiring cosmic energy expanse, had witnessed an epic confrontation between Aidan and Moldark. As the two powerful beings battled for the universe's fate, the celestial bodies surrounding them watched with bated breath, their luminous radiance illuminating the cosmic expanse. The universe's fate hung in the balance for what seemed like an eternity. But finally, with a sense of relief, the Cosmic Nexus seemed to sigh as the cosmic harmony was restored. The celestial bodies resumed their divine dance with renewed vigour, their luminous radiance shining brighter than ever. Aidan and Moldark focused on the Phoenix Stone with the cosmic balance restored. This radiant and powerful crystal pulsed with a sense of contentment as if acknowledging the harmony that had been re-established. The Phoenix Stone had fulfilled its role as a beacon of cosmic equilibrium, bridging the realms of creation and dissolution.

As the Phoenix Stone's guardian, Aidan understood the weight of his responsibility. He vowed to protect it not just for the sake of his world but for the entirety of creation. The Phoenix Stone, with its cosmic significance, was a force of renewal, and he would ensure that its radiance continued to shine as a testament to the enduring power of cosmic balance. With Moldark now an ally, the cosmic order had been preserved, and the delicate harmony of the universe upheld. Aidan's fellowship, each having faced their trials and adversaries, gathered around the Phoenix Stone with a sense of fulfilment. Their unity had been instrumental in safeguarding the cosmic balance, and the bonds forged in the crucible of cosmic battle remained unbreakable.

Ophelia, the ancient forest spirit who had served as Aidan's mentor and guide, walked beside him with a serene and knowing expression. Her presence embodied the essence of renewal and purity, and her wisdom spanned aeons. She spoke with a voice that resonated with profound authority, addressing Aidan and his companions. "You have embraced your destiny," Ophelia said, her words carrying the weight of cosmic truth. "The Phoenix Stone has chosen you as its guardian, and you have proven yourselves worthy of that honour. Your journey has evolved into a cosmic odyssey, a mission to preserve the delicate balance of the universe itself." Aidan nodded with humility, fully aware of his profound responsibility. His role as a Nura'el had expanded into something far more significant—a steward of the cosmic flame, a protector of the Phoenix Stone, and a defender of cosmic order. The radiant energy of the Phoenix Stone pulsed within him, a constant reminder of the universe's enduring potential for renewal.

The fellowship, each member bearing the scars and victories of their cosmic trials, gathered around the Phoenix Stone. Their unity was a testament to the power of collaboration and understanding, a force transcending the boundaries of worlds and dimensions. Together, they represented the enduring spirit of those who sought to protect the cosmic order. With their mission accomplished, the fellowship prepared to leave the Cosmic Nexus. The celestial bodies above offered their blessings, casting a shimmering cascade of stardust that fell like cosmic confetti. It was as though the universe celebrated the restoration of balance and the triumph of light over darkness. Moldark, once a harbinger of darkness, now stood as a protector of cosmic harmony, a living testament to the power of transformation. As they departed, the celestial bodies above seemed to offer their blessings, casting a shimmering cascade of stardust that fell like cosmic confetti. The universe seemed to resonate with their victory, celebrating the restoration of balance and the triumph of light over darkness. The journey of Aidan and his fellowship, which had begun as a quest to protect their world, had evolved into a cosmic odyssey to preserve the very fabric of the universe. Their bonds of destiny had been forged in the crucible of trials and cosmic conflict, and they emerged as heroes of their realm and champions of cosmic order. The Phoenix Stone stood as a testament to the potential for renewal and harmony, even in the face of cosmic discord. It taught those willing to embrace their cosmic responsibilities that the delicate balance of the universe must be protected at all costs. As they gazed up at the stars above, they continued their celestial dance, casting their luminous light upon a universe that had once again found equilibrium. The triumph of cosmic order was a reminder that even the most formidable challenges could be overcome through unity, purpose, and the enduring power of renewal. In the end, they carried with them the enduring lesson of the Phoenix Stone—that even in the face of cosmic discord, the potential for renewal and harmony remained, awaiting those willing to embrace their cosmic responsibilities. The Phoenix Stone's radiance shone as a beacon of hope, inspiring those who sought to protect the delicate balance of the universe and reminding them that, no matter how great the challenge, the potential for renewal and harmony was always within reach.

The legacy they would leave behind would resonate through the ages, a testament to the enduring power of renewal and cosmic balance. Their journey had revealed to them the interconnectedness of all things and the importance of maintaining cosmic harmony. Their victory over Moldark and his malevolent forces had not been a triumph over evil but a reaffirmation of the cosmic order, a restoration of balance that would ripple through the universe. The aftermath of the cosmic clash that had taken place in the Cosmic Nexus was marked by a profound stillness that settled upon the celestial bodies above. The universe had watched the titanic struggle between Aidan's fellowship and Moldark's evil forces. Now, the divine entities shone with a renewed brilliance. It was as though the cosmos had collectively exhaled a sigh of relief, acknowledging the triumph of cosmic order over chaos. Aidan and his fellowship, who had become intertwined with the very essence of the universe, stood as beacons of light amidst the tranquil expanse of the Cosmic Nexus. Their unity had been instrumental in overcoming the formidable adversary that had threatened to disrupt the delicate balance of the cosmos. The fellows fought bravely, using their skills and knowledge to overcome the evil forces that would have destroyed the universe's equilibrium. The Phoenix Stone, the radiant cosmic flame that held the universe's cycles in harmony, pulsed with renewed vigour after the clash. Its luminous energy brightened the celestial battlefield, a testament to the indomitable spirit of those who sought to protect the cosmic order. The Phoenix Stone had fulfilled its role as a beacon of cosmic equilibrium, bridging the realms between creation and dissolution.

The cosmic significance of the Phoenix Stone was no longer confined to the realm of mortals. It had become a symbol of the universe's enduring potential for renewal. This force transcended the boundaries of worlds and dimensions. As its chosen guardian, Aidan understood the weight of the responsibility entrusted to him. His connection to the Phoenix Stone was not merely a duty but a sacred bond that linked him to the essence of creation. Moldark, the once-malevolent adversary who had sought to harness the Phoenix Stone's power for his dark ambitions, had been vanquished. The obsidian armour that had symbolised his dominion over darkness lay shattered and discarded, revealing a form that had been cleansed and purified by the Phoenix Stone's radiant energy. He stood as a living testament to the transformative power of cosmic renewal, a being who had cast off the shackles of malevolence. The fellowship, whose bonds had been forged in the crucible of cosmic conflict, remained united by a shared purpose that extended far beyond their world. They were no longer mortals on a quest; they had become heavenly champions, protectors of the Phoenix Stone's radiant flame, and defenders of the universe's delicate balance. Each member of the fellowship carried the wisdom and strength gained from their trials, and their unity was an unstoppable force.

In the grand tapestry of creation, the Phoenix Stone's radiance shone as a beacon of hope, illuminating the path towards cosmic harmony. As they departed the Cosmic Nexus, the stars above continued their celestial dance, casting their luminous light upon a universe that had once again found equilibrium. The triumph of cosmic order was a reminder that, in the grand tapestry of creation, even the most formidable challenges could be overcome through unity, purpose, and the enduring power of renewal. As Aidan and his fellowship made their way out of the Cosmic Nexus, they carried with them the memory of their epic and gruelling cosmic battle and a profound understanding of their role as guardians of the Phoenix Stone and stewards of the cosmic order. Their journey had evolved into a sacred odyssey that transcended the boundaries of their world, reaching into the very fabric of the universe itself. As they traversed through the cosmic expanse, they faced insurmountable challenges, each one seemingly more daunting than the last. But they had persevered, their unwavering determination fuelled by their shared purpose, their cosmic bond strengthened by their experiences.

TRIALS OF THE HEART

Amidst the cosmic battles and monumental revelations, the journey of Aidan was not devoid of emotional challenges and intricate relationships. As the Nura'el, he was tasked with safeguarding the Phoenix Stone and upholding the cosmic order. Still, the weight of this responsibility often brought him face-to-face with the depths of his emotions and the complexities of his connections with others. Aidan often found himself in moments of quiet contemplation. During these interludes, the weight of his destiny was pressed upon his shoulders with a force that felt as profound as the Phoenix Stone's cosmic radiance. As a cosmic guardian and the protector of the Phoenix Stone, Aidan knew that his role extended far beyond the realm of mortal concerns and carried with it a burden that sometimes felt insurmountable. The Phoenix Stone presence was a constant reminder of the immense responsibility that rested upon his shoulders. It was a duty that resonated with the essence of the universe itself. This responsibility extended beyond the mere preservation of mortal life. It stood before him as a radiant beacon of cosmic energy casting an ethereal and soothing glow.

Despite the clarity of his mission, questions and doubts lingered in the corners of Aidan's mind. As he studied the Phoenix Stone, its pulsating energy seeming to hold the secrets of creation itself, he couldn't help but reflect on the profound cost of his destiny. The emotional toll of knowing that the fate of the universe hinged upon his actions weighed heavily on his heart. It was a burden that transcended the physical and the cosmic—it was a burden of the spirit. The sense of isolation that often accompanied this burden was one of Aidan's most profound challenges. He was acutely aware that his destiny set him apart from the ordinary rhythms of life. While others revelled in the simplicity of their existence, he was tasked with the monumental duty of safeguarding cosmic order. This awareness sometimes left him feeling like a solitary star in the vast cosmic expanse, shining with a unique brilliance but separated from the constellations of ordinary life.

As Aidan sat before the Phoenix Stone, bathed in its transcendent light, he questioned his worthiness. It was not a question born of arrogance or hubris but rather a deep and humble introspection. The Phoenix Stone had chosen him, entrusted with its power, and bound by a destiny that exceeded mortal comprehension. But in the quiet moments, doubt crept in like a whispering shadow. "Am I truly capable?" Aidan wondered aloud, his voice barely more than a whisper in the cosmic silence. "Am I deserving of this responsibility? Can I bear the weight of a destiny that spans the cosmos?" The Phoenix Stone remained unyielding, its radiance a steady and unwavering presence. It did not offer words of assurance, for it was a force of cosmic order, and its wisdom transcended the need for verbal affirmation. Instead, it invited Aidan to seek his answers within the depths of his being. As Aidan's gaze fixed upon the Phoenix Stone, memories of their cosmic battles and triumphs flickered through his mind. He recalled the unity and strength of his fellowship, the enduring spirit of Ophelia, and the wisdom of Mikha'el. These memories were a testament to the resilience of the human spirit, the capacity for growth and transformation, and the enduring power of renewal. Yet, Aidan knew that his path was not one of blind certainty or unwavering confidence. It was a journey marked by vulnerability, introspection, and self-doubt. It was a journey of self-discovery, where the burden of destiny was not meant to break him but to forge him into a guardian worthy of the Phoenix Stone's trust.

As the night stretched on, Aidan remained in communion with the Phoenix Stone. It was a silent conversation, a dialogue of the soul, where questions were asked, doubts were acknowledged, and a sense of purpose was reaffirmed. The Phoenix Stone's radiant energy enveloped him, a reminder that he was not alone in this cosmic endeavour. It was a reminder that the universe itself was a tapestry of interconnected destinies, and his role was but one thread in that grand design. As dawn approached and the first rays of sunlight pierced the horizon, Aidan rose from contemplation. The burden of destiny had not been lifted, but it had been embraced. It was a burden that would continue to shape, challenge, and ultimately define him. And as he stepped away from the Phoenix Stone, he carried with him the knowledge that, in moments of uncertainty, he could always seek solace and guidance in the cosmic radiance of the Phoenix Stone—a beacon of hope and renewal in a universe filled with mysteries and wonders.

Throughout the arduous journey of the Nura'els, the fellowship had grown. The bonds between Aidan and his companions, Lirael, Nalorin, Kaelen, and Ophelia, had grown stronger and closer through the crucible of cosmic battles. They were no longer mere allies united by a common cause but kindred spirits bound together by the unbreakable ties of shared purpose and the indomitable spirit of their quest. The profound camaraderie they shared brought Aidan deep solace, and they found respite in fleeting sanctuaries amid the tempest of their duties. These precious intervals were far more than mere pauses in their journey. They were essential lifelines, offering the fellowship a chance to breathe, reflect, and reconnect with the core of their humanity amid the celestial storms they faced. During these interludes, the true strength of their fellowship was revealed. The Nura'els gathered around a campfire under the vast expanse of a star-studded sky, the weight of their responsibilities seemed to recede momentarily. The ambient crackle of the fire provided a soothing backdrop to their conversations, and the flickering flames danced in harmony with the bonds that had grown between them. The tales they shared spanned the breadth of their lives, delving into the depths of their experiences, hopes, and fears. These stories wove a rich tapestry of shared understanding, transforming their fellowship into a resilient, multifaceted support network. As a thoughtful leader, Aidan often took the initiative to foster these moments of connection. He recognised that the emotional toll of their quest was a burden they all carried, and through these shared stories, they could find solace and strength.

One evening, as the campfire's glow painted their faces with warm, flickering light, Aidan began by recounting a memory from his childhood in the Faelorian Forest. He spoke of the ancient trees and the gentle whispers of the woodland creatures that had been his companions when he was a young boy. He shared how his parents, whose faces were now faded memories, had passed away when he was just a child. Vilem and Elara, Aidan's adoptive parents, had taken him under their guardianship, nurturing him and imparting the knowledge of the forest and Phoenix Stone. They had become his mentor and guide, shaping him into the Nura'el he was destined to be. As he spoke, the gentle crackling of the fire harmonised with the tenderness in his voice. His memories came alive as if the Faelorian Forest had come to life in their midst. His story painted vivid images of his childhood, evoking a sense of nostalgia and longing. Lirael, the enigmatic warrior with a past shrouded in mystery, was the next to share. She spoke of the distant lands from which she hailed, a realm where ancient traditions and a warrior's code were deeply ingrained in her upbringing. Her journey to becoming a Nura'el had been one of self-discovery. This path had led her to embrace her destiny as a guardian of the Phoenix Stone. Nalorin, the ever-curious mage whose inquisitive nature often led them to hidden knowledge, spoke of his fascination with elemental magic. He shared stories of his early experiments with the elemental forces, of the triumphs and mishaps that had marked his path. His boundless curiosity had led him to uncover ancient scrolls and arcane texts that had proved invaluable to their quest. Kaelen, the steadfast and resolute warrior, spoke little of his past but shared his unwavering commitment to their cause. His loyalty to Aidan and the fellowship was unshakable, a testament to the trust that had grown between them. He emphasised the importance of unity and resolve in the face of cosmic challenges. The young forest spirit Ophelia shared tales of her existence. She spoke of her role as a guardian of the Phoenix Stone and the forest's elemental magic. Her stories were imbued with wisdom and a deep reverence for the forces of nature. She recounted how she had chosen to guide and mentor Aidan, recognising the spark of the Phoenix within him.

The night wore on, their shared stories began to weave a collective narrative—a tapestry of experiences, perspectives, and dreams. Laughter and solemn reflection intermingled, creating a symphony of emotions that echoed beneath the starlit canopy. The fellowship found strength and solace in these moments of shared vulnerability and camaraderie. They were no longer isolated individuals facing the vastness of the cosmos alone. They were a united force, bound by purpose and fortified by their shared humanity. Their laughter was a testament to their resilience, a defiant response to the cosmic turmoil they faced. It was a reminder that, even in the face of daunting challenges, the human spirit could find moments of joy, connection, and solidarity. The night was a beautiful reminder of the power of storytelling and the unifying force of shared experiences. The last flames of the campfire dwindled and the cool night air set in, the fellowship members realised that their shared experiences had deepened their connections. Though they still carried the weight of their cosmic responsibilities, they no longer bore the burden alone. Instead, they faced the challenges together, drawing strength from the bonds they had forged around the flickering fire and their shared stories. Amid the celestial tempest, their camaraderie acted as a guiding star, shining bright as a beacon of hope and a testament to the enduring power of unity in the face of cosmic adversity.

Amidst the tumultuous cosmic battles and the weight of their shared destiny, Aidan was entangled in a complicated and profound web of emotions beyond human comprehension. It was a tapestry woven with threads of love, devotion and a cosmic connection that defied all boundaries. Amidst this celestial turmoil, his heart was inexorably drawn towards Ophelia, the wise and ancient forest spirit who had become his mentor and guide. However, the cosmic responsibilities that rested upon their shoulders left no room for personal desires, and the intricacies of their relationship posed a unique challenge. Their love was no ordinary love, for it was unfolding against the backdrop of cosmic forces, the Phoenix Stone's radiant energy, and the grandeur of the universe itself. It was a connection forged in the crucible of their shared purpose. This love transcended the boundaries of mere mortal affection. Theirs was a love story as vast and boundless as the cosmos, unfolding in their cosmic odyssey. Aidan revered Ophelia for her timeless beauty and the profound wisdom and grace that illuminated her every action. Ophelia's unwavering dedication to their mission and her role as a guardian of the Phoenix Stone stirred a deep well of admiration within Aidan. He saw in her not just a mentor and guide but a beacon of hope and a symbol of the enduring spirit of their quest.

Despite the challenges they faced, moments of shared tenderness unfolded in the quiet interludes between cosmic battles. They would steal fleeting moments together under the starlit canopy of the Faelorian Forest or amidst the radiant glow of the Phoenix Stone. In those stolen moments, their love would bloom, transcending the limitations of time and space. However, their love also required profound sacrifice. They had to put the needs of the universe above their desires. Aidan knew that Ophelia, as a guardian of the Phoenix Stone, had responsibilities beyond their relationship. Her commitment to the cosmic order was unwavering, and Aidan respected her duty. Their love was marked by a sense of cosmic connection—a recognition that they were bound together by something greater than themselves. It was a love that found expression in shared glances beneath the celestial tapestry, in whispered words of encouragement amid the turmoil of battle, and in the understanding that their destinies were intertwined with the Phoenix Stone and the universe. In the heart of the cosmic storms they faced, their love was a source of strength and solace. It gave them a profound sense of purpose and a shared resolve to protect the cosmic balance. Their love was not just a personal bond but a cosmic force that fueled their determination to face the challenges ahead.

As the fellowship journeyed through the celestial realms and faced adversaries threatening the fabric of existence, Aidan and Ophelia's love remained a constant, shining like a star in the darkest corners of the universe. It was a love that defied the boundaries of time and space, a love that burned as brightly as the Phoenix Stone itself, and a love that would endure through the ages as a testament to the enduring power of love in the face of cosmic complexity. Amidst the epic journey of the Nura'els, Aidan grappled with a persistent undercurrent of doubt. Despite his unwavering commitment to his role as a guardian of the Phoenix Stone and a steward of the cosmic order, he felt a creeping sense of uncertainty that insinuated his thoughts and emotions. This doubt created a labyrinth of complexity that weighed heavily upon his soul and begged whether he could genuinely fulfil his duties as a Nura'el while navigating the complexities of love and friendship.

The journey itself was a crucible of cosmic battles, where the universe's fate hung in the balance, and the responsibilities of the Nura'els were colossal. Aidan's duty as a protector of the Phoenix Stone and a steward of the cosmic balance extended far beyond the boundaries of the mortal realm and into the very fabric of the universe itself. The consequences of failure were unimaginable, and the fate of creation rested upon his actions and those of his companions. Despite the gravity of his responsibilities, Aidan found himself trapped in the intricacies of human emotion. The bonds of fellowship that had grown stronger with each trial were not merely alliances forged in the crucible of battle; they were the ties of friendship, kinship, and camaraderie. Lirael, Nalorin, Kaelen, and Ophelia were more than allies; they had become kindred spirits bound by a shared purpose. Their laughter shared stories of past adventures, and dreams for the future had become their refuge from the cosmic turmoil surrounding them.

However, the complexity of love weighed most heavily upon Aidan's heart. Ophelia, their mentor and guide, had captured not only his admiration but also his heart. Their love story was no ordinary romance; it unfolded against the backdrop of cosmic forces, the radiant energy of the Phoenix Stone, and the grandeur of the universe itself. It was a connection that transcended the boundaries of mere mortal affection, a love story as vast and boundless as the cosmos. Aidan's admiration for Ophelia ran deep, far beyond the realms of superficial attraction. He revered her for her timeless beauty, indeed. Still, her unwavering dedication to their mission and her role as a guardian of the Phoenix Stone stirred a profound well of admiration within him. With her wisdom and grace, Ophelia was more than a mentor; she was a symbol of hope and the enduring spirit of their quest. Their relationship was not without its complexities. Their cosmic responsibilities were immense, and their duty to safeguard the Phoenix Stone and uphold the universe's balance often took precedence over personal desires. Aidan grappled with the tension between his love for Ophelia and the weight of his destiny. The path of a Nura'el was fraught with sacrifice, and Aidan questioned whether his emotions and attachments were hindrances to his duty.

In the quiet moments of reflection, often under the radiant glow of the Phoenix Stone or beneath the starlit canopy of the Faelorian Forest, Aidan pondered the emotional challenges that weighed on his heart. He yearned for clarity, a way to reconcile the profound emotions that swirled within him with the weighty responsibilities he carried. He wondered whether his love for Ophelia and the bonds of fellowship with his companions were distractions that could cloud his judgment and divert his focus from the cosmic responsibilities he bore. Aidan gazed upon the Phoenix Stone, he marvelled at the radiant energy that emanated from it, casting a warm, otherworldly glow that illuminated the darkness that surrounded him. His thoughts turned to the cost of his duty, and the emotional toll of knowing that the fate of the universe rested upon his actions weighed heavily upon his heart. He questioned his worthiness and the sacrifices that would be required of him. Aidan confronted the very essence of his humanity. He realised that his emotions, far from hindrances, were the core of his existence. Love, friendship, doubt, and even fear were part of the tapestry of human experience, making his journey meaningful. They were not weaknesses to be cast aside but strengths to be embraced. The doubts that tormented Aidan were not merely the product of his inner turmoil. They reflected the more significant question that had haunted the hearts of heroes throughout history—whether pursuing personal happiness, love, and friendship could coexist with the weighty responsibilities of heroism and cosmic duty. As he ventured deeper into the cosmos, Aidan knew that he had to find a balance—a way to honour his emotions without allowing them to jeopardise the cosmic order. He understood that the complexities of love and friendship were not weaknesses but strengths, sources of resilience in the face of adversity. Aidan drew inspiration from the heroes of myth and legend who had faced similar dilemmas. He had found the inner fortitude to prevail. The path ahead was uncertain, and the shadows of doubt would continue to test his resolve. Aidan carried within him the enduring flame of the Phoenix Stone and the cosmic connection that bound him to the universe. He was a Nura'el, not only by duty but by choice, and he was determined to navigate the complexities of his heart while upholding the cosmic balance. The journey was far from over, and the challenges ahead would require courage, strength and the wisdom to embrace the complexities of love and the bonds of fellowship.

Aidan, the Nura'el, found solace in the vast expanse of the cosmos, where the boundaries between realms and worlds were fluid. During moments of solitude beneath the starry canopy of the night, he sought clarity and respite from the immense weight of his destiny. His role as a cosmic guardian transcended the limitations of the mortal realm, and failure to fulfil his responsibilities would have immeasurable consequences. Despite the chaos and conflict of the cosmic battles he faced, Aidan found himself ensnared in the complexities of human emotion. The bonds of fellowship he shared with his companions grew stronger with each trial, and they became more than mere allies. They were kindred spirits bound by a shared purpose, and their laughter, stories, and dreams were their refuge from the turmoil surrounding them. Their love story was not an ordinary romance but a connection transcending the boundaries of mere mortal affection. It unfolded against the backdrop of cosmic forces, the radiant energy of the Phoenix Stone, and the grandeur of the universe itself. The journey also unveiled another layer of Aidan's internal struggle—the shadows of doubt that clouded his judgment. As a cosmic guardian, every decision he made carried cosmic consequences. Doubt was not a luxury he could afford. Yet, it had taken root within him, gnawing at his resolve and challenging his convictions. The emotional challenges weighed heavily on Aidan, threatening to obscure his vision and divert his focus from the cosmic responsibilities he bore. It was a paradox that Aidan grappled with—the juxtaposition of human emotions against the backdrop of cosmic duty. He wondered whether his love for Ophelia and the bonds of fellowship with his companions were distractions that could compromise his judgment and hinder his ability to fulfil his cosmic role.

Aidan understood that love was not a distraction from his cosmic duty but a driving force that fueled his commitment to protect the Phoenix Stone and the universe. With her unwavering dedication, Ophelia was not an impediment to his mission but a source of inspiration and strength. Their love story was not a hindrance; it was a testament to the enduring power of love, even in the face of cosmic challenges.

Friendship, too, was not a vulnerability but a wellspring of resilience. The bonds he shared with Lirael, Nalorin and Kaelen were not distractions but pillars of support that sustained him through the darkest of battles. Their camaraderie and shared laughter were not frivolous diversions but a vital source of comfort and motivation. And doubt, that shadowy spectre that had haunted him, was not a weakness but a tool for discernment. It sharpened his judgment, allowing him to make decisions rooted in wisdom rather than blind certainty. Doubt was a reminder of his humanity, a trait that made him capable of growth and self-reflection. With these realisations, Aidan found a profound sense of resolution within himself. He embraced his emotions and understood they were not adversaries but allies on his journey. They were the colours that painted the canvas of his life, the threads that wove the tapestry of his existence.

The path ahead was still uncertain, and the challenges in wait were formidable. But Aidan faced them with a newfound understanding of the complexities of the human heart and the strength that could be drawn from its depths. Love, friendship, doubt—these tools would guide him in upholding the cosmic balance and protecting the Phoenix Stone. Looking up at the starlit sky, Aidan felt a profound sense of unity with the cosmos. The universe was a tapestry of emotions, energies, and forces beyond mortal comprehension. It was a reminder that even in the face of cosmic duty, the human heart could shine with unwavering resolve.

And so, with his emotions as his compass and his fellowship as his anchor, Aidan embarked on the next leg of his journey. The challenges that awaited him were formidable, but he faced them with a heart unburdened by doubt and a spirit fortified by the complexities of love. His path was illuminated by the radiant glow of the Phoenix Stone, a beacon of hope and cosmic balance that he was determined to protect at all costs. As Aidan embarked on his journey as a Nura'el, he found himself encountering not only external adversaries but also the inner shadows that lurked deep within his own soul. The weight of his responsibilities bore down heavily upon him, and doubts and fears crept up on him like relentless spectres, threatening to extinguish the flames of his resolve.

RESURRECTION'S FLAME

In the quiet of the night, when the stars are distant and untouched, Aidan's inner doubts begin to stir. These doubts aren't fleeting thoughts but rather a gathering of conflicting voices that make him question his own abilities. He wonders if he is truly capable of safeguarding the Phoenix Stone and maintaining order in the vast expanse of the universe or if his expectations are simply unrealistic. These doubts plague Aidan as he looks up at the expansive sky. The enormity of his task and the weight of the universe resting on his shoulders leave him uncertain. He contemplates whether he and his team genuinely possess the skills and fortitude required to undertake such a monumental mission or if they are ordinary individuals with grand aspirations.

Aidan was grappling with a growing sense of uncertainty that threatened to derail his mission. The doubts that plagued him whispered tales of inadequacy and fear of failure, and he found it increasingly difficult to stay focused on the task at hand. As someone who had struggled with doubts before, Aidan knew that they could spiral into something much more insidious if left unchecked. He realised he needed faith in himself and his team to face the challenges ahead, but the doubts made it hard for him to hold onto that belief. He knew that if he succumbed to fear and hesitation, he could jeopardise the entire universe. Aidan was determined to find a way to recapture his confidence to complete his mission and save the lives of those who depended on him.

Aidan sought refuge from the tumultuous thoughts that plagued his mind amid the lush and verdant Faelorian Forest, where the trees towered high, and the air was thick with the sweet scent of nature. This was the place where he had grown up, nurtured and mentored by Ophelia, the wise forest spirit. The forest had always been a sanctuary for him, a place where he could find solace and clarity amidst the chaos of the outside world. As he made his way through the towering trees, his mind drifted to the challenges that lay ahead. Aidan knew that their journey was not for the faint of heart. The battles they had faced and the ones that awaited them were of cosmic proportions. In these moments of reflection, he couldn't help but question his own abilities and limitations.

Did he have what it took to confront the cosmic forces that threatened the universe? The doubts that plagued him cast long shadows over his path, making him wonder if he was indeed equal to the task. He remembered their fierce battles, the moments when victory had hung in the balance, and the cosmic powers that had tested their resolve. Were they truly capable of protecting the Phoenix Stone and preserving the cosmic order? For Aidan, his own abilities as a Nura'el were a constant source of introspection and self-doubt. He had honed his skills over time, mastering the art of tapping into the deeper reserves of his Nura'el abilities with each trial and challenge. But the magnitude of their mission weighed heavily upon him. It wasn't simply about defeating adversaries or mastering elemental forces. It was about understanding the intricate balance of the universe and the cosmic forces that governed it. Ophelia, whose wisdom was as ancient as the forest itself, had instilled in him a deep reverence for the Phoenix Stone, teaching him to draw upon its radiant energy and the essence of the Phoenix. But as he stood beneath the canopy of the Faelorian Forest, the doubts that had plagued him for so long seemed to cast a pall over his connection to the Phoenix Stone.

Aidan's journey had been one of great turmoil, fraught with cosmic battles and encounters with unimaginable forces. The path he had taken was one shrouded in uncertainty, where reality itself seemed to unravel before his very eyes. As he and his companions pressed on toward their goal, Aidan's doubts grew stronger with each challenge they faced. Throughout their journey, Aidan had dug deeper into his Nura'el abilities, seeking to harness the full extent of his powers. However, the inner tempest within him continued to rage on, fueled by his doubts and uncertainties. Even as he made progress, he knew that more challenges lay ahead. The cosmic balance they sought to preserve remained fragile, and the tempest within Aidan mirrored the chaos that threatened to disrupt it. As he grappled with the doubts that echoed in his mind, Aidan's faith in the cosmic order and the importance of their mission began to falter. He questioned whether the universe was truly an uncaring entity that would remain indifferent to their struggles and sacrifices. This crisis of faith was a bitter pill for Aidan to swallow. After all, he had dedicated his life to protecting the Phoenix Stone and maintaining the balance of the universe. Having seen firsthand the destructive consequences of cosmic imbalance, he understood the significance of their mission. But the doubts that plagued him now threatened to undermine the very foundation of his faith.

During moments of doubt, Aidan wondered if their mission was in vain. Were they simply pawns in a cosmic game destined to struggle against insurmountable odds? These questions shook him to his core, leaving him feeling lost and adrift in an uncaring universe. The fellowship of Nura'els, who had once been united in their mission, now found themselves grappling with their own doubts and uncertainties. Lirael, their steadfast warrior, questioned whether her martial prowess was enough to protect the Phoenix Stone against their cosmic adversaries. Nalorin, their mage, doubted the limits of his magical abilities in light of the growing threats they faced. Kaelen, their scout, wondered if her skills were enough to navigate the complexities of their mission. These cracks in their unity were a cause for concern for Aidan. The fellowship had been forged in the heat of cosmic battles, and their bond had been unbreakable. But the doubts that now plagued them threatened to fracture that unity, leaving them vulnerable in the face of their cosmic adversaries.

As the fellowship continued their journey through the vast cosmic expanse, Aidan found himself wrestling with fear in the stillness of night. The campfires flickered like fragile beacons in the vastness of the cosmos, and the distant stars above seemed to hold the answers to questions that weighed heavily on his mind. He had seen the destructive potential of cosmic forces firsthand. He witnessed the malevolence of Moldark and the dark armies that sought to disrupt the cosmic order. Their battles had been nothing short of epic, clashes of elemental might and cosmic significance. And with each confrontation, the stakes had risen higher, the challenges more daunting.

During these quiet moments of reflection, fear crept into Aidan's thoughts like a brooding storm. He wondered whether they were equipped to face the cosmic adversaries ahead. Did they possess the strength, the knowledge, and the unity necessary to safeguard the Phoenix Stone and preserve the balance of the universe? The responsibility they bore was staggering, a burden that threatened to consume them. His concern for his companions compounded Aidan's own fears. Lirael, Nalorin, Kaelen, and Ophelia were more than allies; they were his friends and fellow Phoenix Stone guardians. Their safety weighed heavily on his heart, and the thought of losing any of them filled him with dread.

One of the greatest sources of fear stemmed from the cosmic unknown. With its vastness and complexity, the universe held mysteries that defied comprehension. They were traversing realms and dimensions that few had ever ventured into, confronting adversaries whose powers transcended mortal understanding. The fear of the unknown gnawed at Aidan's resolve. What other cosmic forces lay hidden in the depths of the universe, waiting to challenge them? What cosmic secrets had yet to be unveiled, and what trials awaited them on their quest? The uncertainty of their cosmic mission was a relentless source of fear, a reminder that they were venturing into uncharted territories where the rules of existence differed from anything they had ever known. Perhaps the most daunting aspect of their mission was the weight of cosmic consequences. Aidan understood that their actions had ramifications that extended far beyond the mortal realm. The cosmic balance was a delicate equilibrium, and any disruption could have far-reaching repercussions. Failure was not an option they could afford. The thought of failing to protect the Phoenix Stone and allowing the darkness to seize control of its power filled Aidan with a deep dread. It wasn't just the fate of their world that hung in the balance; it was the fate of the entire universe. The fear of cosmic consequences weighed heavily on Aidan's shoulders. He knew that their mission was a cosmic duty, one that transcended personal desires and individual aspirations. The fate of creation depended on their success, and the thought of failing in that duty was a haunting spectre looming over him. Aidan could only hope that his fears would not overwhelm him and that he could remain steadfast in his commitment to protect the Phoenix Stone and preserve the cosmic balance.

Aidan was confronted with a pivotal decision. Standing at a crossroads, he was faced with two paths: one filled with doubt, leading to an endless cycle of indecision and despair, and the other, filled with determination, leading to an unwavering sense of purpose. As he contemplated his cosmic mission, with all its complexities and challenges, Aidan knew that he needed to commit himself to a steadfast resolve that would transcend any doubts or uncertainties. He understood that doubt would always be a part of the human experience. However, he also knew that it could be harnessed and transformed into a catalyst for strength and determination.

Summoning his courage, Aidan faced the relentless chorus of doubt, determined to silence its dissonant voices. His mission demanded a resolute commitment that would allow him to overcome any obstacles in his path. Drawing inspiration from the stars above, whose distant brilliance served as a reminder of the cosmic order he sought to protect, Aidan reflected on the battles he had fought, the victories he had won, and the unbreakable bonds of fellowship that sustained him. These pillars of his determination served as the foundation upon which he would build his unwavering resolve. With clarity of purpose in his heart, Aidan chose the path of perseverance, knowing that it would guide him through the tempestuous cosmic challenges that lay ahead. He recognised that his mission was not one that he could undertake alone but rather a collective effort and that the unity of his fellowship would be their greatest strength. As he stood firm in his resolve, Aidan felt the echoes of doubt gradually fade away, replaced by a sense of unwavering determination that took root within his heart. It was a determination that would carry him and his companions forward, a beacon of hope that would pierce the cosmic darkness and lead them toward fulfilling their mission. Looking at his fellow travellers, Aidan saw the same spark of resilience and determination in their eyes, forged in the crucible of adversity and uncertainty. He knew that the challenges ahead would be formidable and that doubt would continue to lurk in the shadows. However, he was also confident that their unyielding spirit and unwavering determination would see them through the most trying of times.

As the leader of the fellowship, Aidan was not only responsible for his actions but also for the well-being and morale of his companions. He felt a heavy burden of leadership, compounded by his fear of making the wrong decisions and leading his companions into danger. This fear haunted him constantly, and he questioned his capability to guide them through the cosmic challenges they faced. The doubt in his leadership abilities was a constant shadow that he struggled to dispel.

As Aidan grappled with his inner turmoil, Ophelia, the wise and radiant mentor of the fellowship, sensed his internal conflict. She recognised the signs of doubt and fear clouded his spirit, for she had faced such challenges in her journey as a Nura'el. With a grace that seemed to emanate from the Phoenix Stone itself, Ophelia approached Aidan, her presence like a soothing balm that enveloped him. Ophelia was a beacon of serenity during their cosmic battles and the weighty responsibilities they carried. Her company had a calming effect, a reminder that amidst the chaos of their mission, a core of tranquillity could be found. Ophelia had been a mentor and guide to countless generations of Nura'els. She understood their tumultuous journey, the doubts and fears that could threaten to unravel even the strongest spirit. Ophelia's appearance often seemed like an extension of the Phoenix Stone's radiant energy. Her skin bore an ethereal glow, and her eyes shone with the luminescence of ancient wisdom. She moved with a grace that hinted at a profound connection with the cosmic forces, a connection that Aidan and his companions could only aspire to. When she approached Aidan, she did so not as an all-knowing teacher but as a compassionate guide who had faced her moments of doubt. Her understanding was not born of detached wisdom but personal struggle and growth. One of the most potent aspects of Ophelia's guidance was her willingness to share her vulnerabilities. She spoke of times when she had questioned her worthiness as a guardian of the Phoenix Stone when the burden of cosmic responsibility had felt overwhelming. Her openness created a space for Aidan and the fellowship to acknowledge their doubts without shame. Through her stories of resilience and determination, Ophelia conveyed that doubt was not a sign of weakness but a crucible through which one's resolve could be forged.

Her experiences served as a testament to the idea that there was a path forward even in moments of most profound uncertainty. Ophelia often wove cosmic perspectives into her guidance. She spoke of the Phoenix Stone as a cosmic artefact, a fragment of the universe's essence. She explained that their mission as Nura'els was about safeguarding a relic and upholding the balance of the cosmos. This cosmic perspective helped Aidan see his doubts and fears in a new light. They were no longer mere personal struggles but part of a cosmic tapestry of challenges faced by those who sought to protect the Phoenix Stone and the universe.

Ophelia's guidance instilled a sense of purpose that extended far beyond his concerns. With her words and presence, Ophelia created a space of safety and compassion for Aidan and his companions, helping them to find the courage and strength to face the challenges ahead. Throughout his journey as a Nura'el, Aidan received guidance from Ophelia, whose teachings were profound and transformative. Ophelia's direction was centred around the weight of cosmic responsibility that Aidan and his companions carried as protectors of the Phoenix Stone, a source of power and heavenly anchor that sustained the balance of creation and dissolution. Ophelia didn't shy away from acknowledging the immense burden that the Nura'els carried. She spoke of the consequences of failure, not to instil fear but to underscore the gravity of their mission. She emphasised the strength of their fellowship as a source of resilience. She reminded Aidan that they were not alone in their cosmic struggle. Each company member brought unique powers and abilities to the table, forming a cohesive unit greater than the sum of its parts.

One of Aidan's most profound lessons from Ophelia was that fear could be transcended. She didn't dismiss Aidan's doubts and fears; instead, she framed them as integral parts of the celestial symphony. Just as the universe underwent cycles of creation and dissolution, so did the human spirit experience cycles of doubt and determination. Aidan found a new way of understanding his inner turmoil in this cosmic perspective. Ophelia explained that fear was a natural response to the enormity of their mission. However, it didn't have to dictate their actions. It could be acknowledged, understood, and then transformed into courage. Her journey had been a testament to this transformation, having faced cosmic adversaries and witnessed the darkest cosmic imbalances. Yet, she emerged with a spirit that radiated light. Her presence proved that fear could be transmuted into a force for good. Through Ophelia's guidance, Aidan understood that hope was not a fragile emotion but a wellspring of resilience. It was the belief that despite their cosmic challenges, there was always a path forward. Ophelia's unwavering hope in the face of adversity became a well of inspiration for Aidan. Her stories of triumph over seemingly insurmountable odds reminded him that their mission was not a futile endeavour. It was a testament to the indomitable spirit of those who dared to protect the Phoenix Stone and uphold the cosmic balance.

In that moment, beneath the canopy of stars, Aidan and his companions made an unspoken vow, united in their commitment to confront doubt with determination, face uncertainty with courage and resolve, and stand together in their cosmic mission. The chorus of doubt may still linger in the background, but it would no longer hold sway over their actions. As they continued on their cosmic journey, Aidan and his companions were emboldened by the strength of their determination, ready to face whatever trials the universe had in store for them. Once distant and indifferent, the stars above now shone with a renewed brilliance, casting their radiant light upon a fellowship bound by determination and unbreakable resolve. And so, with their hearts ablaze with determination, Aidan and his companions pressed on, knowing that their unyielding spirit would see them through whatever challenges lay ahead. Doubt may continue to whisper in the background. However, it could no longer hold them back, for their strength was born of an unwavering determination and an unbreakable spirit. Aidan's mind was consumed by doubts that had been sown, and the seeds of anxiety and trepidation had taken root. The cosmic battles that loomed on the horizon cast long shadows over his spirit, and fear had become a constant companion. The enormity of the task that lay ahead, the magnitude of their adversary's power, and the cosmic consequences of failure all conspired to awaken the spectre of fear within him.

Aidan knew that fear, if left unaddressed, could strain the bonds of their fellowship. He was grappling with his fears and wondered if his companions were experiencing similar emotions. The weight of responsibility, the strain of their cosmic mission, and the ever-present fear of failure could erode the unity that had been their greatest strength. Aidan's fear extended to his relationships within the fellowship as well. He worried that his anxieties might unintentionally affect his interactions with his companions. The fear of letting them down or not living up to their expectations was a constant source of unease. Amid cosmic battles and trials, Aidan's fear manifested as a tempest within him, threatening to engulf his determination and resolve. The cosmic storms they faced were mirrored by the storm of emotions that raged within his heart and mind. Aidan understood that he had to confront his fear, to find a way to harness it and turn it into a source of strength rather than weakness. The path ahead was treacherous, and there was no room for fear to dictate their actions. Despite the shadows of fear, Aidan found a glimmer of hope. He realised that fear could be a powerful motivator when acknowledged and confronted. It could drive them to prepare more diligently, to seek a greater understanding of the cosmic forces they faced, and to strengthen their bonds of unity.

Aidan knew it was natural to feel fear in the face of such monumental challenges. It reminded them that their mission was of cosmic significance, a duty that demanded their utmost dedication and determination. And so, with fear as their companion, Aidan and his fellowship prepared to face the cosmic unknown with courage and resilience, ready to confront the tempests that lay ahead and emerge stronger on the other side. Throughout his tumultuous internal struggles, Aidan sought refuge under the starry expanse of the night sky. In these moments of tranquil contemplation, he found an unexpected companion in the vast cosmos. As he gazed up at the celestial tapestry, he felt an otherworldly connection that transcended the boundaries of the mortal realm. With its boundless wisdom and unfathomable vastness, the cosmos appeared to offer a sanctuary from the constant doubts and fears that plagued him. Aidan envisaged the stars as ancient entities that had observed the rise and fall of civilisations, and their constancy became a source of comfort. Under the infinite canvas of the night sky, Aidan often found himself drawn into a state of profound introspection. He would lie on the cool ground, his eyes locked on the stars that adorned the heavens. In those moments, he felt small yet connected, a mere speck in the grand tapestry of the cosmos. The stars, resembling beacons of ancient wisdom, whispered secrets of the universe to Aidan. Their silent presence, punctuated by the occasional streak of a shooting star, held a timeless reassurance. He began to perceive the cosmos as a repository of cosmic knowledge, a silent observer of the ebb and flow of existence.

Aidan began having inner conversations with the stars as he gazed at them. He envisioned each star as a vessel of wisdom, a celestial sage who had witnessed galaxies unfolding, stars' birth and death, and the cosmic dances that shaped the universe. During these imaginary dialogues, Aidan would pour out his doubts, fears, and questions to the stars. He would speak of the burden of his destiny, the weight of cosmic responsibilities, and the challenges ahead. In the stillness of the night, he found a space where his innermost thoughts could be shared without judgment. Although he knew the stars could not provide conventional answers, he felt that their silent presence and imagined wisdom bestowed a form of solace. It was as though the cosmos, in its vastness, could absorb his worries and fears, helping him gain a new perspective on his role as a guardian of the Phoenix Stone and the cosmic order. The act of stargazing became a form of heavenly contemplation for Aidan. It enabled him to step outside his thoughts and immerse himself in the larger mysteries of existence. He would ponder the nature of the universe, the cycles of creation and dissolution, and the cosmic forces that shaped reality.

Aidan's fears and doubts began to lose their oppressive weight in these moments. With its infinite expanse, the cosmos reminded him that his struggles were but a small part of a grander narrative. It encouraged him to embrace the uncertainties of his mission as an integral part of the cosmic design. One of the profound realisations that Aidan gained from his cosmic contemplations was a shift in perspective. He began to see his fears and doubts as part of the human experience—a reflection of the vast spectrum of emotions that the cosmos might encompass. The universe, he reasoned, was not just a realm of cold, unfeeling forces; it was a tapestry of experiences, including the profound emotional journeys of beings like himself. This perspective helped Aidan make peace with his internal struggles. He recognised that fear and doubt were not weaknesses but aspects of his humanity. They were the shadows that contrasted the brilliance of hope and determination. Just as the cosmos held light and dark within it, so did his own heart. Aidan's connection with the cosmos made him perceive the universe as a living symphony of energies. Each celestial body, each cosmic phenomenon, played a unique role in this cosmic orchestration. It reminded them that their mission, as Nura'els, was part of this more excellent cosmic symphony.

The Phoenix Stone held the essence of the Phoenix's magic and was like a harmonious note within the cosmic composition. Aidan understood that their duty was not to dominate or control the cosmic forces but to harmonise with them, to ensure that the Phoenix Stone's radiant energy contributed positively to the cosmic balance. Aidan gazed up at the starry night sky and couldn't help but feel a sense of wonder and awe. The beauty and vastness of the cosmos never failed to amaze him. In these quiet stargazing moments, he found a sense of clarity and peace that eluded him in his day-to-day life. For Aidan, the stars were more than just celestial bodies; they were a source of inspiration and guidance. Whenever he felt lost or uncertain, he would turn to the cosmos for solace and direction. The silence of the night beneath the cosmic expanse offered a form of meditation that allowed him to tune out the noise and distractions that often plagued his mind. Through stargazing, Aidan discovered the value of stillness and silence. In these moments of quiet contemplation, he felt a deep connection to the universe that transcended words. It was as though he was communing with the cosmos, tapping into a source of wisdom and guidance beyond language and rational thought. As he gazed at the stars, Aidan began to understand the concept of cosmic time. He realised that the stars he saw in the night sky were not static but part of a dynamic, ever-changing cosmic dance. They moved through the heavens, their positions shifting over millennia. This understanding of cosmic time offered Aidan a perspective on his journey. He saw that his challenges were moments in the grand continuum of existence.

Over time, Aidan's communion with the cosmos became a source of resilience. It was as though the stars infused him with a sense of cosmic purpose. He carried the wisdom of the cosmos within him, a reminder that his mission as a Nura'el was part of a larger cosmic plan. Despite his fears and doubts, Aidan learned to navigate them with more excellent stability. He no longer saw them as insurmountable obstacles but as challenges to be embraced and understood. Just as the stars persisted in their luminous existence despite the cosmic chaos around them, so could he persevere as a guardian of the Phoenix Stone. Ultimately, the cosmos became Aidan's confidante, a silent companion who witnessed his inner struggles. While the stars couldn't provide definitive answers, their presence offered a sense of cosmic camaraderie. They reminded him that, in the grand scheme of the universe, his journey was a meaningful and integral part of the cosmic story. Underneath the tapestry of stars, Aidan found solace in the knowledge that he was not alone in his cosmic odyssey. The universe itself was his confidante, and the silent communion he shared with the cosmos provided a sense of connection that transcended the boundaries of the mortal realm. In the vast expanse of the night sky, he discovered a source of strength, wisdom, and cosmic reassurance that helped him confront the tempests within and emerge as a guardian of the Phoenix Stone with renewed resolve.

Aidan continued receiving Ophelia's guidance and noticed a transformation within himself. His doubts, while still present, no longer held him captive. Instead, they became catalysts for growth and self-discovery. He realised that doubt was not a signal to abandon his mission but an invitation to deepen his understanding of himself and the cosmos. Through introspection and guidance from Ophelia, he learned to embrace doubt as a teacher rather than a tormentor. Ophelia's role as a mentor extended beyond words. Her presence was a source of inspiration, embodying the qualities of a guardian of the Phoenix Stone. She radiated a sense of purpose and cosmic wisdom that Aidan and his companions could draw strength from. In her, Aidan saw the embodiment of what a Nura'el could become: someone who carried the weight of cosmic responsibility with grace and resilience. Her radiant heart illuminated the path ahead, reminding him that the journey, with all its doubts and challenges, was worth undertaking. Aidan continued his journey. He knew his bond with Ophelia would endure. She had become more than a mentor; she was a cosmic companion who guided him through the darkest cosmic storms. Her lessons would continue to resonate within him, reminding him that doubt and fear were not obstacles but threads in the cosmic tapestry of his destiny. Ophelia's guidance had been an invaluable source of heavenly wisdom that had transformed Aidan's understanding of himself and his place in the universe.

Ophelia guided Aidan on a journey of self-reflection. Together, they delved into the recesses of his mind, exploring the shadows that held him captive. With gentle guidance, Ophelia encouraged Aidan to confront his doubts and fears, acknowledging that they were not enemies to be defeated but aspects of his humanity. As they settled into the serene environment, Ophelia encouraged Aidan to close his eyes and turn his gaze inward, guiding him into deep introspection. The Phoenix Stone's energy resonated harmoniously with one's innermost thoughts and feelings, amplifying his awareness and offering protection and support.

With Ophelia's guidance, Aidan began visualising his doubts and fears as shadowy figures lurking in the corners of his consciousness. Each doubt took on a distinct form; each fear had a unique presence. They appeared as spectres of uncertainty and anxiety, whispering their dissonant truths. Some questioned his worthiness as a guardian of the Phoenix Stone, while others painted vivid scenarios of cosmic catastrophe. These shadows were the very embodiment of his inner turmoil. Through this process of introspection, Aidan began to understand that doubt and fear were not absolute truths but interpretations of past experiences and future uncertainties. They were narratives he had woven in his mind; like any story, they could be rewritten. Fear, too, came under scrutiny. Aidan examined the nature of his fears and found that they often revolved around the unknown and the potential consequences of their mission's failure. They were projections of the mind, magnified by the cosmic scale of their responsibilities.

Ophelia guided him in recognising that fear was a primal response, a survival mechanism that had evolved over aeons. It was not inherently harmful but needed to be understood and harnessed. As Aidan continued to explore the depths of his consciousness, he uncovered a profound truth—the vulnerability of courage. He understood courage was not the absence of fear or doubt but the willingness to act despite them. Through this process of self-reflection, Aidan learned the healing power of acceptance. He acknowledged that doubt and fear were not enemies to be conquered but facets of his experience. They were part of the cosmic dance of emotions that enriched his journey. With Ophelia's support, he practised self-compassion, treating himself with the same kindness and understanding he extended to his companions. He realised that by accepting his doubts and fears, he could transform them into sources of strength. Aidan delved deeper into self-reflection and embraced the cosmic paradox—that strength and vulnerability could coexist. He saw that the greatest heroes in the cosmic tapestry had faced their doubts and fears with courage, not by denying them but by integrating them into their cosmic journey. The Phoenix Stone's presence amplifies this paradox, reminding him that the artefact held the balance between creation and dissolution, strength and vulnerability, doubt and determination. It was a symbol of the cosmic dance that defined all existence. Throughout this journey of self-reflection, Aidan found that the cosmos itself was a mirror for his inner world. The vastness of the universe reflected the vastness of his consciousness. Like distant suns, the stars represented the myriad thoughts and emotions that dwelled within him. In the cosmic expanse, he saw the interconnectedness of all things, the tapestry of existence woven from threads of doubt and determination.

In the arduous journey of self-discovery, Aidan delved deep within himself and uncovered the source of his inner strength. He realised that doubt, when confronted with unwavering determination, could be transformed into a powerful catalyst for growth. When met with courage, fear could be harnessed as a source of resilience. This profound transformation within himself marked a significant turning point for Aidan. He recognised that the path of a Nura'el was not a journey devoid of doubt or fear but rather one that necessitated the triumph of the spirit over these shadows. It was about rising above adversity, similar to the mythical Phoenix, and emerging stronger and more resilient. This realisation acted as a forge, tempering Aidan's resolve and commitment to his mission. The doubts that once held him captive were now the fires that fueled his determination. The fears that once cast shadows over his path now served as beacons, guiding him through the cosmic storms ahead. Determination became Aidan's guiding star, a force that transcended mere resolve. It was an unwavering commitment to protect the Phoenix Stone and preserve the cosmic order, even amid uncertainty and adversity. Determination coursed through his veins with each step forward like a potent elixir. It was the driving force behind his actions, the fuel that propelled him through the cosmic battles that awaited. Aidan understood that his doubts and fears were not weaknesses but stepping stones toward mastery.

Once a shadow that cast doubt upon his abilities, fear was now harnessed as a source of strength. Aidan had learned to acknowledge his concerns without allowing them to paralyse him. Instead, he used them as reminders of the importance of their mission and the dire consequences of failure. Fear became a motivator, a guardian that kept him vigilant and prepared. It was a primal instinct that heightened his senses and sharpened his awareness in the face of danger. Aidan had come to respect fear as a cosmic force that, when channelled wisely, could lead to remarkable feats of courage. Doubt, too, underwent a profound transformation. It was no longer a shroud of uncertainty but a catalyst for growth and self-improvement. Aidan had learned that doubt was often a reflection of the desire to excel, to question the status quo, and to seek higher levels of mastery.

He welcomed doubt as a teacher, a cosmic guide that urged him to delve deeper into his abilities and understanding. Doubt spurred him to explore new horizons and discover untapped reservoirs of potential. It was a reminder that growth and self-discovery were ongoing processes in the cosmic journey. Aidan's commitment to his role as a Nura'el became unwavering through the forging of resolve. He knew that their mission to protect the Phoenix Stone and preserve the cosmic order was not a simple task but a profound cosmic responsibility. It was a duty that transcended personal doubts and fears. Aidan's commitment extended beyond himself to his companions, the world, and the universe. He saw their fellowship as a united front against the forces of darkness, a beacon of hope in a cosmos filled with uncertainty. Together, they would forge a path through the cosmic battlefield, their determination a shield against the adversities ahead. As Aidan's inner transformation unfolded, he realised that his journey was not a solitary endeavour but part of a cosmic symphony. Each member of the fellowship contributed notes to this symphony—notes of determination, courage, and resilience. Together, they created a harmonious melody that resonated through the universe itself. Their commitment to the cosmic order was like the conductor's baton, guiding the symphony of existence. Doubt and fear were not discordant elements but integral parts of the composition. They added depth and texture to the symphony, making it a masterpiece of cosmic proportions. The journey of a Nura'el was not just about defeating evil; it was about creating a symphony of hope, courage, and resilience that echoed throughout the cosmos.

Aidan's journey as a Nura'el was a profound odyssey that took him through the depths of his psyche. Doubt and fear were integral to his path, and he learned to embrace them as cosmic forces within the human spirit. Doubt and fear were like opposing forces, each challenging him to confront the boundaries of his comfort zone, to question the certainties he held, and to explore the depths of his courage. For Aidan, the first step in cosmic dance was acknowledgement. He had to recognise and accept the presence of doubt and fear within himself. This was not a sign of weakness but an act of self-awareness. By acknowledging these shadows, he could begin to understand their origins and their role in his journey. Aidan had noticed that doubt would sneak up on him occasionally. It would creep in from a place of vulnerability and start whispering tales of inadequacy. It would remind him of past mistakes and failures and make him question his abilities. However, Aidan soon realised that doubt, in its way, was a reflection of his desire to excel. It was a reminder that growth and self-discovery were ongoing processes and that he could always strive to reach higher levels of mastery. Despite its sometimes unsettling nature, doubt had become a trusted companion on his journey towards personal growth. Fear, too, had its roots in self-preservation. It was an ancient instinct that had evolved to protect living beings from harm. Aidan came to respect fear as a primal force that, when channelled wisely, could lead to remarkable feats of courage. The cosmic guardian kept him alert and prepared in the face of cosmic battles. Once acknowledged, doubt and fear became partners in a heavenly dialogue.

Aidan conversed with these inner forces, seeking to understand their messages and discern their truths. Doubt's questions became invitations to introspection, to examine his motivations and aspirations. Aidan was a person who took heed of the warnings that fear presented to him. Fear served as a beacon for him, urging him to stay alert and prepare for whatever challenges lay ahead. He realised that fear was a guiding light that directed him towards self-preservation and wise decision-making. Through his experiences, Aidan learned to distinguish between rational and irrational doubts. He acknowledged that not every doubt he had was a legitimate critique of his abilities, as some were born out of unwarranted fears or external influences. By engaging in a cosmic dialogue with his inner self, he could discern which of his suspicions were worth addressing and which were mere distractions on his path.

The next phase of the dance was harnessing doubt and fear as catalysts for growth and transformation. Aidan realised these forces were not meant to hinder him but to propel him on his cosmic journey. Doubt, when channelled wisely, could be a catalyst for self-improvement. It encouraged him to explore new horizons, question assumptions, and delve deeper into his abilities. Doubt was the cosmic teacher that challenged him to evolve and strive for excellence. Fear, when transformed into courage, was a wellspring of resilience. Aidan embraced fear as a source of motivation, a reminder of the importance of their mission. Fear heightened his senses and sharpened his awareness, making him more vigilant in the cosmic battles that lay ahead. The latter emerged as the cosmic conductor in the cosmic dance of doubt and courage. Courage was not the absence of fear or doubt but the unwavering commitment to move forward despite their presence. The force propelled Aidan through the cosmic storms that challenged their fellowship.

With every step forward, courage coursed through Aidan's veins like a potent elixir. It was the driving force behind his actions, the fuel that propelled him through the cosmic battles. Aidan understood that courage was not the absence of doubt or fear but the triumph of the spirit over these shadows. The cosmic dance of suspicion and courage was not confined to Aidan alone. Each member of the fellowship contributed their notes to this symphony. Doubt, fear, courage, and determination were like musical elements, each adding a unique timbre to the composition. As Aidan delved deeper into his inner journey, he realised that the interplay of doubt and courage was a never-ending cycle. It wasn't a one-time act but an everlasting cosmic ballet. Despite journeying into the unknown, he knew that doubt and fear would always arise, but he had the strength to overcome them. He danced through the cosmos with bravery in his heart and doubt by his side, embracing both the light and the shadows and uncovering the enigmas ahead.

The Guardians of the Phoenix Stone

PHOENIX'S SACRIFICE

Aidan's long and arduous journey drew closer to its ultimate destination, and a pivotal moment of heartbreaking sacrifice arose, fundamentally reshaping his perception of love, loyalty, and the immense potential harbouring within the Nura'els. This was a moment of profound reckoning, where the strength of personal connections would be put to the test, and the fate of the universe hung precariously in the balance. Such was the gravity of the situation that even the slightest misstep could have catastrophic consequences, making it imperative that Aidan and his comrades tread carefully and make the right choices.

Aidan and Ophelia found themselves in the heart of the Celestial Oasis and were struck by the incredible beauty surrounding them. The stars above twinkled like diamonds in the sky, casting gentle light upon the lovers as they stood in awe of their surroundings. The cosmic night was alive with colour, a breathtaking tableau that seemed to shift and change before their eyes. The Celestial Oasis was a place of wonder, existing in a space between dimensions where the veil between realms was thin. It was a place where the cosmic energies flowed freely, creating a breathtaking picture of the grandeur of the universe. The stillness of this place was palpable, pregnant with cosmic potential, and the stars themselves seemed to pause in awe of the moment that was about to unfold. As Aidan and Ophelia stood amid this celestial splendour, they gazed into each other's eyes with a love that needed no words. Their bond was born of shared experiences and a profound connection with the Phoenix Stone and the cosmic order. Their souls, intertwined like cosmic threads, had found solace and completeness in each other's presence.

For Aidan, Ophelia was not just a mentor and guide but also the beacon of light that guided him through the darkest cosmic storms. Her wisdom, grace, and unwavering dedication to their mission had illuminated his path. He saw the embodiment of the Phoenix Stone's radiant energy in her—a force of renewal and hope. Ophelia, in turn, had watched Aidan's growth with a heart brimming with pride and affection. She had nurtured his potential, guiding him to embrace his destiny as a Nura'el. The bond they shared was not only one of love but of shared purpose—a commitment to safeguard the cosmic order and protect the Phoenix Stone. Their love was not without its cosmic challenges. The very fabric of the universe held a complexity that sought to test the depth of their connection. The duties of a Nura'el were all-encompassing, and their mission to protect the Phoenix Stone and preserve the cosmic order was arduous. Yet, amidst the chaos of cosmic battles and the weight of their responsibilities, Aidan and Ophelia had found moments of solace and connection. They had shared stolen moments beneath the starlit skies, where the cosmic energies seemed to harmonise with their love. These moments were like cosmic interludes, where time slowed to allow them to savour the depth of their emotions.

In the Celestial Oasis, Aidan and Ophelia stood at the nexus of their destiny, surrounded by the very energies that had forged their bond. The cosmic stars, those ancient witnesses to the universe's grand narrative, cast their benevolent gaze upon the pair to acknowledge the significance of their love. It was in this hallowed space that Aidan's heart swelled with a profound realisation. Their love was not merely a personal connection but a cosmic force in its own right. It was a love that defied the boundaries of time and space, transcending the mortal realm to become a part of the universe's narrative. As he gazed into Ophelia's eyes, he saw the same realisation mirrored in her gaze. Their love was not a distraction from their cosmic responsibilities but embodied them. It was a testament to the enduring power of love in the face of cosmic challenges. Even as they stood entwined by the cosmic forces, a weighty decision loomed. Aidan and Ophelia knew their love, as powerful as it was, came with its cosmic consequences. The duties of a Nura'el were all-encompassing, and their passion could either fortify their resolve or become a heavenly distraction.

In the depths of that moment, as the stars bore witness to their connection, Aidan understood the gravity of the choice before him. He knew he had to decide whether to allow their love to flourish, become a source of strength, or temper it in the fires of duty, safeguarding the cosmic order above all else. Aidan found himself in a dilemma that tested the boundaries of his duty and love. It was not a matter of choosing between one and the other but a complex symphony that aimed to achieve harmony between these two profound forces. However, as he pondered on their journey, he realised that their love had been a guiding star that illuminated their path towards fulfilling their cosmic duty. It had equipped them with the strength to face unimaginable challenges and the resilience to endure even during cosmic storms.

Aidan and Ophelia stood united in a love that transcended the mortal realm. As they stood in the heart of the Celestial Oasis, the cosmic forces that flowed through this ethereal sanctuary seemed to pause as if acknowledging and blessing the profound union that had blossomed between them. With its timeless wisdom and boundless mysteries, the universe appeared to embrace their love. It was as though the very cosmos had given a gentle sigh, a cosmic exhalation that signified approval and recognition. The stars that adorned the cosmic tapestry twinkled with a flash of subtle brilliance, their radiance accentuating the depth of Aidan and Ophelia's connection. It was as if the stars were applauding their love a love that had not weakened their cosmic duty but had become an integral part of it. Ophelia's smile conveyed a depth of understanding that transcended words. With a simple gesture, she placed her hand upon Aidan's chest, over his heart, symbolically touching the very source of their love. Her touch was a silent acknowledgement, a profound expression of the belief that their love was not a distraction from their cosmic duty but a testament to its enduring power.

The Celestial Oasis had become a witness to their love, a place where the boundaries between realms grew thin. The cosmic energies courting through this sanctuary had woven a tapestry of approval, enveloping them in its radiant embrace. Their love had not detracted from their mission but fortified their resolve, lending them the strength to face the challenges ahead. Upon bidding farewell to the Celestial Oasis, Aidan and Ophelia were imbued with a profound sense of spiritual serenity. Their bond, steeped in a love transcending the physical realm, had become integral to their cosmic voyage. It served as a beacon of hope and unwavering strength, propelling them forward in the face of formidable challenges. The universe had blessed them with a divine connection that would accompany them on their journey through time and space. As they gazed upon the vastness of the cosmos, their relationship grew stronger and more profound. They were sure their love would serve as a guiding light, illuminating their journey through life. This bond was not bound by the limitations of time and space; instead, it was a celestial force as mighty and awe-inspiring as the stars surrounding them.

As they took each step forward, the profound love shared between them served as a poignant reminder of the interconnectedness of all things within the vast and intricate design of the universe. This powerful and all-encompassing love only strengthened their unwavering commitment to protect the Phoenix Stone and preserve the very fabric of cosmic order. They understood that love was an integral part of the universe's intricate and harmonious design and that it possessed a cosmic force all its own. It was a love that transcended time and space and embodied the very essence of the universe itself. As they embarked on their cosmic journey, Aidan and Ophelia knew their love would continue to burn brightly amidst the cosmic tapestry. It would be a source of strength and inspiration as they faced the challenges ahead. Their love was not a hindrance but a cosmic force—an embodiment of the universe's intricate design, where love and duty danced together in heavenly harmony. As he gazed upon the scene before him, Aidan felt a sense of awe and wonder wash over him. It was as if the universe had opened before him, revealing a vision that would forever remain etched in his memory. The moment's beauty was overwhelming, and Aidan felt his heart swell with emotion as he witnessed a profound and heart-wrenching vision unfolding. It was a moment that would stay with him forever, a testament to the power of love and the majesty of the cosmos. The vision was not a mere daydream or fleeting illusion—it was something deeper and more profound. It was as if the very fabric of the cosmos had opened up to reveal a tapestry of interconnected events, threads of destiny that wove together the past, the present, and a potential future. Each line represented a pivotal moment, a choice made, or an action taken, and all of them converged upon a single, heart-rending moment.

Aidan's eyes scanned the unfolding scene before him, his heart leapt with awe and wonder. There, standing steadfastly before the illustrious Phoenix Stone, was his beloved Ophelia. The gemstone dazzled brilliantly in the light, its radiant hues casting a hypnotic spell on all who beheld it. Its essence seemed to emanate outwards, imbuing the surrounding area with a deeply ingrained sense of cosmic order. Ophelia's unwavering gaze remained fixed upon the Phoenix Stone with an unyielding determination, her hand raised in intense concentration. Aidan could sense the sheer power and energy coursing through her body as if she were a conduit for the very forces of the universe. She was engulfed and enveloped in a sudden burst of cosmic energy, forming an ethereal shield around her body, the likes of which had never before been seen. Aidan stood transfixed, his breath caught in his throat as he watched in amazement. He knew this was a moment of great significance, a pivotal moment in the history of their world. And through it all, Ophelia remained steadfast and resolute, her gaze never wavering from the Phoenix Stone. It was a sight that would stay with him forever, a moment of pure magic and wonder that he would never forget.

Aidan watched in awe as he realised that Ophelia sacrificed herself to protect the Phoenix Stone. She was absorbing an immense and devastating cosmic force, a cataclysmic energy that threatened to disrupt the very balance of the universe. However, she consumed it with grace and selflessness, fully aware of the dire consequences if she failed in her duty. As Aidan witnessed the vision unfolding before him, emotions overwhelmed him.

A deep sense of love enveloped him, yet a tinge of fear, sorrow, and awe lingered within him. It was clear to him that he was faced with a significant decision that would not only determine his fate but the fate of the universe as a whole. He carried the weighty responsibility of deciding whether or not to embrace the vision as a possible future. In doing so, he would have to make the ultimate sacrifice and allow Ophelia to safeguard the Phoenix Stone, preserving the delicate cosmic balance. The gravity of the situation weighed heavily on him, and he knew that his decision would have far-reaching consequences that could shape the future of all existence.

The decision at hand carried a weight that surpassed the bounds of his understanding as if it were an all-encompassing force that bore down upon him heavily. He found himself torn between love and obligation, both of which seemed to demand the ultimate sacrifice. On the one hand, he could choose to embrace the situation before him, but in doing so, he would be forced to endure the excruciating pain of watching the love of his life willingly surrender herself for the greater good. It was a choice that demanded much of him, and he could not make it lightly. He was acutely aware of the immense power and significance of the love he shared with his partner, a force recognised and sanctified by the cosmos. However, he also realised the gravity of their responsibility as Nura'els, as they were the guardians of the Phoenix Stone, entrusted with maintaining the equilibrium of the universe. This was a task that was equally profound and significant, adding to the complexity of his decision-making process.

Aidan was presented with a daunting and complex dilemma that posed a threat to his love and obligations. He found himself in a state of inner turmoil as he struggled to maintain the purity of his affection while fulfilling his responsibility to maintain the delicate equilibrium of the universe. This was an immense burden that no one should ever have to bear, but the fate of the cosmos rested squarely on his shoulders, and he knew that he had to make a decision that would have far-reaching consequences. As Aidan locked eyes with Ophelia, he felt a sense of awe wash over him. Her unwavering gaze spoke volumes about the strength of her spirit, and he knew that he had found a kindred soul. It was clear that she had caught a glimpse of their possible future together, and her commitment to him was nothing short of inspiring. As they stood under the starry night sky, he couldn't help but feel grateful for her unwavering dedication to upholding universal harmony. The constellations above twinkle with approval as if affirming the depth of their connection. It was as if time stood still, and they both knew they were destined to be together. The ambience of the Celestial Oasis was profoundly tranquil as if the entirety of existence was holding its breath in anticipation of Aidan's decision. The weight of destiny, love, and the harmonious workings of the cosmos all seemed to converge upon him, compelling him to choose a path that would impact his own life and the very fabric of the universe. Aidan was acutely aware of the far-reaching implications of his choices, and he could sense the heavy burden of responsibility bearing down on him, threatening to crush him under its weight. The enormity of the situation was not lost on him, and he knew that the universe's fate was inextricably tied to the decision he was about to make.

Aidan was left in utter awe by the grandeur of the cosmic sanctuary that surrounded him. The striking contrast between the turbulent storm of emotions brewing within him and the breathtaking beauty of his environment was palpable. The vast expanse of his consciousness seemed to be a battleground for emotions such as love, despair, doubt, and fear, each vying for dominance like cosmic forces competing for control. The oasis seemed to be a facade, concealing his inner turmoil. Despite the tranquillity of his surroundings, the chaos within him was evident, and he couldn't help but feel like a mere speck in the vastness of the universe.

Doubt and uncertainty began to creep into Aidan's mind, whispering insidious questions that eroded the foundations of his resolve. Could he allow Ophelia to make such a sacrifice? Was their love worth the cosmic consequences of her gift? Were they truly capable of fulfilling their roles as Nura'els, safeguarding the Phoenix Stone and preserving the cosmic order?

These questions were corrosive, eating away at his clarity and paralysing him from making a decision. The fear of cosmic consequences, rather than physical harm or battle, weighed heavily on his shoulders. He understood that the universe hung in the balance and any disruption could have far-reaching ramifications. Amidst this tempest of emotions, Aidan found himself standing at a crossroads that transcended the personal and delved into the heart of cosmic duty. Each emotion carried its weight, its significance, and its consequences. Love, despair, doubt, and fear swirled and clashed like cosmic elements in an intricate dance.

Aidan knew he could not escape this tempest; he could only navigate it with the wisdom and strength the universe bestowed upon him as a Nura'el. The weight of his decision was great, but he knew that with faith in their love and the cosmic order, he and Ophelia could fulfil their duty and preserve the universe's balance. Amidst the turbulence of his emotional state, Aidan found solace in gazing upwards towards the vast expanse of the cosmos. The Celestial Oasis, adorned with shimmering celestial lights, was a breathtaking backdrop for his moment of reflection and transcendence. As he looked up at the stars, which had existed since ancient times as witnesses to the unfolding cosmic drama, Aidan felt as though they offered their silent wisdom to him in his troubled state.

As Aidan gazed upon the stars, he contemplated the sacrifices that had been made throughout the ages to maintain the cosmic balance. Planets collided, stars collapsed, and galaxies merged—all in the name of cosmic equilibrium. These sacrifices were on a scale that transcended human comprehension and paved the way for the existence of life itself. In the grand cosmic tapestry, every act of sacrifice, whether by celestial bodies or sentient beings, was a thread that contributed to the greater design. Aidan understood that their mission as Nura'els reflected this cosmic principle—a willingness to sacrifice even the most cherished aspects of existence to preserve the greater whole. The wisdom of Ophelia, their mentor and guide, echoed in Aidan's mind. She had always emphasised the interconnectedness of all life, the delicate web of existence that bound together the smallest organism and the mightiest star. Her teachings stressed the importance of balance, harmony, and selflessness in the face of cosmic duty.

Ophelia had often recounted tales of cosmic events, of stars going supernova to disperse life-giving elements across the cosmos, of planets aligning to create gravitational forces that shaped entire solar systems, and of comets blazing through the sky, leaving behind the seeds of life on fertile worlds. These stories had not just been lessons; they had been glimpses into the greater cosmic narrative.

In the celestial expanse, the stars appeared to become more than distant specks of light. They witnessed the struggles and choices of those who sought to protect the cosmic order. The rise and fall of civilisations, the birth and death of stars, and the unfolding of countless destinies had been observed by the stars in their timeless existence. The stars held a perspective that transcended the limitations of human emotions and desires. Aidan felt a profound connection to the universe as he contemplated the stars above. It was a reminder that their love, sacrifices, and choices were part of a greater cosmic narrative. The universe itself had conspired to bring them together and offered blessings upon their union. The vision he had witnessed was not merely a glimpse into a possible future. It was a testament to the universe's acknowledgement of their love and its understanding of the cosmic responsibilities they bore.

The weight of the moment was palpable as a vision of Ophelia's sacrifice hung heavy in the air. It was a glimpse into a future where her essence would merge with the Phoenix Stone, safeguarding the cosmic balance. Aidan had known that this moment was coming, but the reality still hit him like a ton of bricks. He took a deep breath, his chest heavy with the weight of the decision he had to make.

Aidan's voice trembled with emotion as he spoke, "Ophelia, the vision has shown us the path we must take. Your sacrifice is the key to preserving the cosmic harmony."

Ophelia, her eyes filled with love and understanding, nodded in response to Aidan's words. She had always been a beacon of wisdom and grace, and now, in the face of this heart-wrenching choice, she exemplified the very essence of her teachings—a willingness to sacrifice personal desires for the greater good of the cosmos.

"Aidan," she said, her voice resonating with cosmic truth, "our love is bound by the cosmic tapestry. We are but threads in the fabric of the universe, and sometimes, threads must be sacrificed to mend the tapestry."

Her words held a profound wisdom—a recognition that their love, while powerful and enduring, was part of a greater cosmic narrative. In the grand design of the universe, personal desires sometimes had to yield to the imperative of the greater whole. It was a lesson Ophelia had imparted throughout their journey, and now, it was a lesson they would embody.

Aidan and Ophelia shared a final, heart-wrenching embrace, sealing their fates in the cosmic order. It was a moment that transcended the mortal realm, a moment where love and sacrifice became one. Their connection, forged through trials and cosmic battles, had prepared them for this ultimate test. The Celestial Oasis bore witness as Ophelia, with a serene grace that defied the turmoil in her heart, began to walk towards the Phoenix Stone. Each step brought her closer to the radiant energies that emanated from the sacred artefact. Her form, bathed in the cosmic glow, seemed to merge with the very essence of the Phoenix Stone. Aidan watched in awe and sorrow as Ophelia's figure gradually dissolved into the shimmering brilliance of the Phoenix Stone. It was a sight that filled him with profound grief and reverence. His love for Ophelia, their shared journey, and the cosmic responsibilities they had shouldered were all encapsulated in this moment. As Ophelia's presence became one with the Phoenix Stone, Aidan felt a surge of energy—a harmonious resonance that emanated from the artefact. It was as if the Phoenix Stone acknowledged the sacrifice and welcomed Ophelia's essence into its cosmic embrace.

The celestial lights in the Oasis seemed to shine brighter, their radiance spreading across the tranquil waters and illuminating the entire sanctum. The cosmic forces that pulsed through the Phoenix Stone vibrated with a renewed vitality, a testament to the sacrifice that had been made. In the wake of this cosmic transformation, Aidan remained standing by the Phoenix Stone, his heart heavy with grief but also with an unwavering commitment to the cosmic balance. He knew that Ophelia's sacrifice was not in vain; it was necessary to ensure the preservation of the universe's harmony. With Ophelia's sacrifice, a new chapter in their cosmic journey had begun. Aidan knew the road ahead would be filled with challenges and trials, but he carried the enduring love they had shared and the wisdom Ophelia had imparted. It was a love that transcended time and space and was woven into the very fabric of the universe.

After Ophelia's sacrifice, the Celestial Oasis was enveloped in a profound stillness that seemed to reverberate throughout the cosmos as though the universe held its breath in anticipation of what would come. Standing alone by the Phoenix Stone, Aidan was consumed by an all-encompassing grief that threatened to overwhelm him. He had watched, with a mixture of sorrow and awe, as Ophelia's physical form dissolved into the radiant energies of the Phoenix Stone, her essence becoming one with the cosmic tapestry. The depth of his loss was immeasurable, and Aidan struggled to accept that his guide, mentor, and beloved had willingly sacrificed herself to safeguard the universe's balance. Ophelia's selflessness and unwavering commitment to the greater good had left an indelible mark on his soul, and he knew that he would carry that mark with him for the rest of his existence. As he stood there, lost in grief, Aidan felt he was holding vigil over the Phoenix Stone, the very heart of the Celestial Oasis. The radiant energies that pulsed through the Phoenix Stone seemed to flicker and dance in his vision as though they were alive with a renewed vitality. At that moment, he understood that Ophelia's sacrifice had not been in vain; it was necessary to ensure the preservation of the universe's harmony. The Celestial Oasis, once a place of serenity and contemplation, had been transformed into a sacred sanctuary where their destinies had been interwoven with the greater cosmic narrative. Aidan felt an overwhelming sense of unity with the universe itself. It was as though the cosmos had embraced him, acknowledging the love, sacrifice, and dedication he and Ophelia had embodied.

Just when Aidan thought all hope was lost, a phenomenon of cosmic proportions unfolded before his eyes. From the ashes of Ophelia's sacrifice, a phoenix emerged—an ethereal being bathed in celestial light, its wings stretching wide to embrace the entire universe. Aidan's heart skipped a beat as he recognised the being before him—it was Ophelia, transformed and transcendent. The Phoenix Stone's flames had not consumed her; she had been reborn. Her essence, now interwoven with cosmic energies, radiated a brilliance rivalling the stars.

The phoenix Ophelia hovered in the air, a vision of cosmic beauty and power. Her presence defied mortal understanding, for the limitations of the physical realm no longer bound her. She was a guardian of the Phoenix Stone, a cosmic entity, and a testament to the incredible power that flowed within the Nura'els' bloodline. A profound realisation washed over him as Aidan gazed upon the transformed Ophelia. The vision he had witnessed—the sacrifice, the merging with the Phoenix Stone, and the rebirth as a phoenix—had been a glimpse into the cosmic order's intricate design. It was a revelation that transcended mortal comprehension.

Ophelia had become a living embodiment of the Phoenix Stone's power, a guardian of the cosmic flame, and a bridge between the mortal and celestial realms. Her sacrifice had not extinguished her existence but had elevated her to a higher astral plane. She was now a cosmic force of boundless wisdom and radiant energy.

With awe and reverence, Aidan reached out to Ophelia, who descended gracefully to meet him. Her form radiated warmth and serenity, and her eyes held the wisdom of ages. Their hands touched, and Aidan felt a connection transcending mortal boundaries at that moment.

"Ophelia," he whispered, his voice filled with love and wonder, "you have become something beyond mortal understanding."

She smiled a smile that held the essence of galaxies and the secrets of the cosmos. "Our love," she replied, "is no longer bound by the constraints of mortality. It is a love that spans the expanse of the universe, a love that endures across time and space."

As the cosmic revelation settled within Aidan's heart, he understood their journey had taken on a new dimension. Ophelia, now a guardian of the Phoenix Stone and a celestial being, had not left him but had become an integral part of his cosmic legacy. Their hands reached out to each other, fingers intertwining as if they were merging not just their physical forms but their very souls. The cosmic forces surrounding them seemed to acknowledge their love with a gentle sigh as if the universe approved of this union. This union strengthened their resolve rather than weakened it.

With a profound sense of unity and purpose, Aidan and Ophelia shared a cosmic embrace. Their hearts, once burdened by the weight of sacrifice, now beat in unison with the universe's rhythm. They had become more than mortal lovers; they were cosmic beings, guardians of the Phoenix Stone and stewards of the cosmic order.

Together, they would continue their mission as Nura'els, protecting the Phoenix Stone and upholding the universe's balance. Aidan knew they faced challenges and trials that transcended the mortal realm, but they were an unstoppable force with Ophelia in her cosmic form by his side. Their love, once a flame that burned brightly in the mortal world, had now become a cosmic fire, a beacon that illuminated the path ahead. As they soared through the Celestial Oasis, two heavenly beings bound by love and destiny carried the enduring legacy of the Nura'els. This legacy had been tested, transformed, and reborn in the fires of the Phoenix Stone. In the aftermath of the profound cosmic transformation that had taken place in the Celestial Oasis, Aidan and Ophelia found themselves reunited. Their love had transcended the limitations of the mortal realm, becoming a force that defied time and space. They stood together, surrounded by the soft, shimmering light of the cosmic stars, as a profound sense of unity with the universe enveloped them. Their love had undergone a metamorphosis, transforming from mere mortal affection to a cosmic force that bound them to the Phoenix Stone, cosmic harmony, and each other. As they looked into each other's eyes, they saw the reflection of their shared history and the promise of a future far beyond their existence

Standing together in the Celestial Oasis, bathed in the celestial light of the cosmic stars, Aidan and Ophelia understood that their love was not a distraction from their cosmic duty but a testament to its enduring power. Their union had not weakened their commitment to the universe but had fortified it. Their love illuminated the path ahead, guiding them through the awaited challenges and trials. They were ready to continue their mission as Nura'els, for they knew their love was now a cosmic force—an integral part of the universe's grand design.

With a renewed sense of purpose and an unbreakable bond forged in the cosmic flames of the Phoenix Stone, Aidan and Ophelia prepared to face the cosmic challenges ahead. Their love, once a flame that burned brightly in the mortal world, had now become a heavenly fire, a force of renewal and harmony that would forever burn like a beacon in the infinite expanse of the cosmos. Together, they would protect the Phoenix Stone, uphold the universe's balance, and carry forward their enduring legacy as Nura'els—a legacy of love, sacrifice, and cosmic destiny. Their passion had transcended the limits of the mortal realm, becoming a cosmic force that would forever bind them to the Phoenix Stone and each other as they journeyed forward into the unknown depths of the universe.

REBIRTH FROM ASHES

After the epic battle and the stunning transformation of Ophelia, the universe of Aidan and the fellowship underwent a profound metamorphosis. The cosmic energies unleashed during their ordeal left an indelible mark, reshaping the physical realm and the essence of their mission and understanding of the universe. In the aftermath of the cosmic transformation that had taken place in the Celestial Oasis, the world seemed to be reborn. The once tumultuous and tempestuous energies that had surged through the Phoenix Stone had now found their equilibrium, and a profound serenity settled upon the land.

The natural world, in particular, underwent a striking transformation. The plants and trees that inhabited the oasis had transformed their own. The once-struggling flora now flourished with a vitality that seemed otherworldly. Their leaves shimmered with iridescent hues, and their blooms emitted a soft, celestial glow. It was as if they had absorbed the essence of the Phoenix Stone's cosmic flames, and this newfound energy had breathed life into every fibre of their being. The animals that roamed the oasis had also experienced a resurgence. Their movements were graceful, and their interactions seemed imbued with a sense of harmony. The once-tense predator-prey relationships had been replaced with a delicate balance within the ecosystem. It was as if the cosmic transformation had renewed individual creatures' vitality and harmonised their relationships.

The skies above the Celestial Oasis had undergone a breathtaking transformation. After the transpired cosmic events, the heavens seemed to shimmer with an ethereal brilliance. The stars that adorned the night sky appeared more radiant than ever, their twinkling lights a testament to the cosmic forces that governed the universe. The moon, which had once cast a blood-red hue upon the landscape, now glowed with a serene, silvery light. Its phases mirror the balance and harmony restored to the world below. It no longer bore the ominous warning it once had; instead, it radiated a sense of cosmic serenity.

For Aidan and Ophelia, who had borne witness to the transformation of the Phoenix Stone and the rebirth of the universe, the changes in the world around them were a testament to the enduring power of their mission as Nura'els. The Phoenix Stone's cosmic flames had preserved cosmic harmony and renewed and revitalised the world. As they stood in the heart of the Celestial Oasis, they could feel the cosmic energy that pulsed through the land. It was a force that bound them to the Phoenix Stone, a power that flowed within their very beings. They were no longer mortals on a quest; they had become stewards of the cosmic order, and the world acknowledged their role in the universe's grand design. The transformation of the Celestial Oasis reflected the broader changes that had occurred in the universe. The cosmic energies that had once teetered on the precipice of chaos were now in perfect equilibrium. The delicate balance between creation and dissolution, life and death, had been restored. The Phoenix Stone radiant energy, which had surged with tempestuous power during the cosmic confrontation, now burned with a steady, radiant glow. It symbolised the Nura'els' unwavering commitment to preserving the cosmic order.

As Aidan and Ophelia gazed at the transformed Celestial Oasis, they knew their journey was far from over. The world had been reborn, but their duty as guardians of the Phoenix Stone and protectors of the cosmic harmony continued. The universe had granted them a second chance to uphold the balance sustaining all creation. With renewed determination and an unbreakable bond forged in the cosmic flames of the Phoenix Stone, Aidan and

Ophelia prepared to face the challenges ahead. They understood that the universe was in a state of perpetual renewal, and their role as Nura'els was to ensure that this cosmic dance continued, preserving the harmony and balance that were the essence of existence.

Aidan and Ophelia embarked on the next phase of their cosmic journey in the heart of the reborn universe amidst the radiant flora, harmonious fauna, and shimmering celestial skies. This journey would test their resolve, challenge their understanding, and reaffirm their love as a force transcending time and space. The world was now a place of unparalleled beauty, where cosmic energy flowed freely and harmoniously, and the Nura'els were the guardians of cosmic harmony, ensuring that the universe remained in perfect balance. The events that transpired in the Celestial Oasis profoundly impacted the members of the fellowship of Nura'els. Aidan and Ophelia's transformation was a cosmic miracle that transcended mortal comprehension. The fellowship's journey, already fraught with cosmic challenges and revelations, took on an entirely new dimension as they bore witness to Ophelia's rebirth. This event reshaped their understanding of the universe and their place within it.

The bonds between the fellowship members had always been strong, forged through countless battles and shared moments of triumph and adversity. However, the rebirth of Ophelia deepened those connections to a level beyond mortal comprehension. They now shared a cosmic link, an intricate tapestry of understanding and purpose that bound them together inextricably. Lirael, the steadfast and resourceful fellowship member, found herself contemplating their newfound cosmic awareness. Her sharp intellect had always served her well in deciphering the mysteries of the Phoenix Stone and the Phoenix's magic. Now, she felt an even stronger connection to the celestial forces that governed their mission. The cosmos seemed to whisper its secrets to her, and she listened with a sense of reverence, eager to unravel the profound truths it held. Nalorin, the enigmatic and perceptive member of the fellowship, had always possessed an innate ability to perceive cosmic energies and foresee potential futures. This gift had guided them through treacherous situations. After the rebirth of Ophelia, Nalorin's insights deepened. He could now sense the delicate balance of the universe with greater clarity, enabling him to anticipate cosmic disturbances and threats before they fully manifested. Kaelen, the brave and determined member of the fellowship, had been a pillar of strength in their battles against darkness. Her unwavering courage had often been the driving force behind their victories. Now, she felt an even greater responsibility to protect the cosmic order. The heavenly flames of the Phoenix Stone burned within her, infusing her with a purpose that extended beyond their world. She became a beacon of cosmic strength, inspiring her companions to rise to the challenges ahead. And then there was Aidan, the central figure of the fellowship and the Nura'el, whose journey had been marked by profound revelations and inner growth. His connection to the Phoenix Stone had evolved into something cosmic, a wellspring of cosmic energy that flowed through him. He had transcended his mortal limitations, becoming a guardian of the Phoenix Stone and a steward of cosmic harmony. Aidan was now a leader and a celestial beacon, guiding his companions in their mission to protect the Phoenix Stone.

The rebirth of Ophelia also deepened the fellowship's understanding of the cosmos. They had witnessed firsthand the incredible power of the Phoenix Stone and its role as a cosmic anchor. The Phoenix Stone was not merely a source of magical energy but a beacon of cosmic balance, a nexus point where the forces of creation and dissolution converged. This newfound understanding allowed them to perceive the universe in a different light. They realised that their mission as Nura'els was not confined to the mortal realm but was intricately woven into the fabric of the cosmos. They were now custodians of the cosmic order, tasked with preserving the delicate balance sustaining all creation.

As they journeyed through the transformed world of the Celestial Oasis, they could sense the cosmic energies that pulsed through the land. The rejuvenated flora and fauna served as a testament to the universe's resilience and capacity for renewal. Every blade of grass and whispering breeze seemed to resonate with the cosmic harmony they had helped restore. The fellowship understood that

126

their role as Nura'els had evolved into something greater than they had initially imagined. They were no longer novices on a dangerous quest but cosmic champions, chosen by destiny to safeguard the Phoenix Stone and preserve the universe's balance. Their cosmic connection amplified their strengths and abilities, making them a formidable force against any cosmic threats that might arise. Together, they embodied the harmonious interplay of heavenly forces—creation and dissolution, light and shadow, life and death. As they looked to the future, the fellowship of Nura'els embraced their cosmic destiny with unwavering determination. They knew that their journey was far from over and that the universe's cosmic dance would continue, with them as its guardians and stewards. Each step they took, each challenge they faced, was a testament to their commitment to the enduring cosmic harmony that bound them together, forging a legacy that would resonate through the ages.

The rebirth of Ophelia as a cosmic being marked a new chapter in the history of the fellowship of Nura'els. No longer was she just their mentor, for she had now become a living embodiment of the power of cosmic transformation and the enduring legacy of their mission. Her wisdom, grace, and newfound abilities radiated like a celestial beacon, guiding the fellowship towards a destiny transcending their world's boundaries. Ophelia's transformation had resulted in her becoming a cosmic entity interwoven with the very essence of the universe. Her physical form was now a manifestation of the radiant energy of the Phoenix Stone, and her presence exuded a sense of cosmic authority. The fellowship was in awe of Ophelia's newfound abilities. She could harness the cosmic forces that flowed through her, channelling them with precision and grace. Unlike mortal magic, her abilities were not limited by the constraints of the physical world, for she wielded the cosmic energies with an innate understanding of their intricate dance. Thanks to her mastery over the Phoenix Stone's cosmic magic, Ophelia could protect it in ways they had never imagined. She could create celestial barriers to shield the Phoenix Stone from evil forces and tap into its power to restore cosmic balance when disturbances threatened to disrupt it. Her cosmic awareness allowed her to sense cosmic disturbances across the universe, ensuring they could respond swiftly to any threats.

Ophelia's rebirth also elevated her role within the fellowship. She was now their cosmic guide, more than just a mentor. Her guidance went beyond the practical aspects of their mission as she delved into the profound mysteries of the cosmos, helping the fellowship understand the intricate web of cosmic forces that governed their world. Under her tutelage, the fellowship gained a deeper understanding of the Phoenix Stone and its connection to the universe. They learned to attune themselves to the cosmic energies, enabling them to harness its power more effectively. Ophelia's teachings were not limited to spells and incantations; she imparted heavenly wisdom that transcended the mortal realm. Ophelia's unique position as a living conduit of cosmic energy allowed her to act as a guardian of the Phoenix Stone in ways that no one else could. She could commune with the Phoenix Stone on a cosmic level, understanding its needs and desires. This deep connection enabled her to ensure that the Phoenix Stone remained in perfect harmony with the universe.

The fellowship's mission had become more significant than they had initially imagined. They were not just protecting a magical artefact but upholding the cosmic balance itself. Ophelia's role was pivotal in this endeavour, as her cosmic insights allowed them to anticipate cosmic disturbances and take proactive measures to preserve harmony. Ophelia's transformation profoundly impacted the fellowship's perspective on mortality and legacy. They understood that their roles as Nura'els were not confined to their lifetimes but were part of an enduring cosmic legacy—Ophelia's existence as a celestial being served as a testament to the enduring nature of their mission. The fellowship realised their actions had repercussions far beyond their individual lives. They were stewards of a legacy that spanned aeons, responsible for maintaining the cosmic harmony for generations. Time constraints did not bind their dedication to the Phoenix Stone and the universe but were a commitment to an eternal cosmic order. As they continued their journey, guided by Ophelia's wisdom and cosmic insight, the fellowship of Nura'els embraced their role as astral guardians. They became threads in the grand tapestry of the universe, each thread crucial to maintaining the cosmic balance. Their understanding of the Phoenix Stone, the Phoenix, and the cosmos deepened with every revelation, and they strove to align their actions with the greater cosmic design.

Ophelia's legacy was a testament to her transformation and a reminder of the interconnectedness of all life within the universe. The cosmic forces that flowed through her reflected the same forces that governed the stars, planets, and all living beings. The fellowship's journey was about protecting the Phoenix Stone and participating in the cosmic dance of creation and dissolution, ensuring that the universe continued to thrive in perfect harmony. The revelation of Ophelia's transformation brought about a significant shift in the purpose and perspective of the Nura'els. Once regarded as the only protectors of the Phoenix Stone, their mission now extended beyond the realm of their world, encompassing the preservation of cosmic harmony and the balance of the entire universe. The Phoenix Stone, once the centre of their quest, had taken on a much grander purpose, becoming a symbol of a greater mission that extended far beyond their immediate surroundings. Upon realising the implications of Ophelia's transformation, the fellows grappled with the weight of their newfound responsibilities.

Their journey, which had initially been focused on the terrestrial realm, had transcended into the cosmic domain, and they were stewards of the very forces that governed the universe itself. This called for a deeper understanding of the intricate web of cosmic energies and celestial forces that permeated the cosmos, and the fellowship understood that their knowledge and skills had to evolve to meet this broader cosmic challenge. Ophelia played a pivotal role in their cosmic education as their astral guide, imparting wisdom that delved into the fabric of creation. She allowed the fellowship to appreciate the Phoenix Stone's intrinsic magic and vital role in the balance of celestial forces.

Ophelia's transformation had allowed her to commune with the Phoenix Stone on a profound cosmic level. She understood its role as a linchpin in the cosmic order and recognised that it held the key to preserving harmony throughout the universe. Under her guidance, the fellowship learned to appreciate the Phoenix Stone's significance and vital role in balancing celestial forces. The fellowship had evolved from being mere guardians of a relic to becoming protectors of cosmic harmony. Their actions and choices now had repercussions that resonated across the cosmos, and they were responsible for safeguarding the delicate equilibrium of celestial bodies, cosmic energies, and the very essence of creation. Their expanded responsibility meant they had to be vigilant and attuned to cosmic disturbances, imbalances, and threats to the universal order. With Ophelia's cosmic awareness, they could sense disturbances that might otherwise go unnoticed, allowing them to respond swiftly and effectively. Ophelia's transformation had woven the fellowship into the very fabric of the universe. They became cosmic threads, each contributing to the intricate tapestry of cosmic harmony. Their roles were not defined by individual desires or aspirations but by the imperative of cosmic balance.

Just as the Phoenix Stone served as a nexus, so did the fellowship, connecting the mortal realm with the cosmic forces that governed the universe. Their journey reflected the greater cosmic dance of creation and dissolution, cosmic order and chaos. They were tasked with ensuring that this dance continued in perfect harmony. The fellowship realised that their mission was not confined to their lifetimes. Their roles as stewards of cosmic harmony extended beyond the limitations of time and mortality. They were part of a legacy that spanned aeons and demanded unwavering dedication to preserving the universe's balance. This commitment to the cosmic order was a solemn oath, a promise to uphold the universe's balance regardless of personal sacrifices or hardships. The fellowship understood that their actions echoed through the annals of cosmic history and that their choices had far-reaching consequences that affected their world and countless others across the cosmos.

Ophelia's transformation had ignited a cosmic awakening within the fellowship, and they were determined to honour their role as guardians of the universe's harmony. Their challenges were no longer localised; they were cosmic, demanding a level of understanding, courage, and sacrifice that stretched their abilities to the limits. Yet, they were resolute in their commitment to the greater good, ready to face whatever cosmic trials lay ahead in their quest to preserve the celestial harmony of the universe. The incredible voyage of Aidan and his fellowship was a cosmic odyssey that extended far beyond the boundaries of their world. As they ventured deeper into the vast expanse of space, they encountered awe-inspiring celestial beings and cosmic phenomena that exceeded the limits of human understanding. Their exploration of the universe became a pilgrimage, revealing the grandeur and complexity of the cosmic tapestry.

With their redefined purpose and cosmic responsibilities, the fellows embarked on a journey transcending their world's boundaries. Their quest was no longer limited to protecting the Phoenix Stone; it encompassed the preservation of cosmic harmony and the equilibrium of celestial forces. They sought to ensure that the universe continued to thrive in perfect balance, upholding the cosmic order that had endured since immemorial.

One of the most remarkable aspects of their journey was their encounter with celestial beings. These entities possessed immense power and wisdom, existing beyond the mortal realm. They were the guardians of cosmic knowledge, protectors of heavenly secrets, and timeless observers of the universe's grand design. Conversations with these celestial beings were profound and enlightening. They shared insights into the nature of creation, the ebb and flow of cosmic energies, and the delicate balance that held the universe together. Aidan and the fellowship deepened their understanding of their cosmic responsibilities through these interactions. Cosmic phenomena played a vital role in their journey, opening their eyes to the universe's wonders. They witnessed the enigmatic dance of black holes, where the laws of physics seemed to bend and warp in mysterious ways. The event horizons of these cosmic entities served as gateways to other dimensions, reminding them of the infinite mysteries that awaited discovery in the cosmos.

Nebulae, vast interstellar dust and gas clouds, revealed the cosmic nurseries where stars were born. Aidan and his companions were captivated by the breathtaking beauty of these stellar birthing grounds, where the forces of creation were at work. It reinforced their understanding that their mission was to protect and nurture the processes of cosmic renewal. One of the most profound experiences during their cosmic exploration was their ability to communicate with ancient stars. These celestial entities witnessed civilisations' rise and fall, the birth and death of worlds, and the eternal cosmic cycle of creation and dissolution.

Conversations with ancient stars were like journeys through time and memory. They shared stories of cosmic events that spanned aeons, narrating the epic sagas of celestial battles, cosmic alignments, and the continual evolution of the universe. Aidan and the fellowship learned that they were not alone in their quest to safeguard cosmic harmony; they were part of a timeless heavenly tradition upheld by the stars themselves. Perhaps the most profound and humbling experiences occurred when they bore witness to the birth and death of galaxies. They observed the majestic spectacle of galaxies forming, their swirling masses of stars and cosmic dust coalescing into brilliant spirals or ellipticals. These heavenly birthing grounds were like celestial cradles, where the promise of new worlds and civilisations ignited.

Conversely, they also witnessed the sombre, majestic spectacle of galaxies in their twilight years, where stars burned out, and the remnants of once-vibrant civilisations faded into cosmic oblivion. The death throes of galaxies were reminders of the impermanence of all things in the cosmos and the eternal cycle of creation and renewal. As Aidan and the fellowship journeyed through the cosmos, they began to perceive the universe as a vast and interconnected tapestry. Each celestial body, cosmic event, and stellar entity contributed to this intricate weave, forming a symphony of energies and forces that sustained the cosmic order. They realised that their roles as Nura'els were not confined to their world alone. Their mission encompassed the entire cosmos, and they were threads in this cosmic tapestry. Their actions resonated within their world and throughout the universe, influencing the balance of celestial forces and the harmony of creation itself. Aidan and the fellowship understood the profound interconnectedness of all life by exploring the cosmic tapestry. They saw how the birth and death of stars influenced the evolution of worlds, how the energies of black holes shaped the cosmic landscape, and how the actions of celestial beings reverberated through the ages. This understanding deepened their commitment to their cosmic responsibilities. They realised that their actions, no matter how small, played a part in the greater cosmic dance. Just as every thread was essential to the integrity of a tapestry, so were their roles vital to preserving the celestial harmony of the universe.

A revelation dawned upon Aidan and his companions as their journey continued—the universe itself was a living entity. It breathed, evolved, and possessed a cosmic consciousness transcending mortal comprehension. They understood their quest was not a battle against an adversary but a harmonious collaboration with the universe's grand design. This perspective transformed their approach to their mission. They no longer saw themselves as mere defenders but co-creators in the cosmic symphony. They sought to align their actions with the universe's natural rhythms, honouring the ebb and flow of cosmic energies and contributing to the greater cosmic harmony. The echoes of the major battle and Ophelia's transformation had far-reaching consequences that reverberated throughout the cosmos. The impact was profound, extending beyond the immediate aftermath and leaving an enduring mark on the universe. As Aidan and the fellowship continued their journey, they were acutely aware that they were stewards of a universe that had undergone a transformation that would shape the course of cosmic events.

The consequence of their victory in the earlier battle was preserving the cosmic balance. Moldark's malevolent ambitions had been thwarted, and the delicate equilibrium that held the universe together had been safeguarded. However, restoring the Phoenix Stone's rightful place as a beacon of cosmic balance and renewal had far-reaching effects. Its luminous presence influenced the celestial forces, ensuring that creation and dissolution continued their eternal dance without disruption. The Phoenix Stone had become a symbol of hope and a testament to the enduring power of cosmic order. The universe itself had transformed, resonating with the aftermath of the major battle. Once in turmoil, the cosmic forces had found equilibrium, and the celestial bodies moved in graceful synchrony. It was as if the universe had breathed a sigh of relief, acknowledging the triumph of cosmic order over chaos. This cosmic harmony extended to every corner of existence. Worlds flourished with vitality, celestial phenomena unfolded with serenity, and the cosmic ballet of creation and dissolution flowed without impediment. The skies above shimmered with a radiant brilliance as if the stars themselves celebrated the restoration of balance. Aidan and the fellowship had evolved into something greater than mortal beings. Their experiences had transcended the boundaries of the ordinary, and they had become cosmic guardians with a profound understanding of the universe's intricacies. Their trials had forged them into vessels of heavenly wisdom and strength.

Their odyssey was a testament to the fact that in the face of cosmic challenges, the unity of purpose, the power of love, and the triumph of courage could reshape the cosmos' destiny. With every step they took, Aidan and the fellowship continued to inscribe their legacy into the annals of cosmic history, ensuring that the universe remained a place of beauty, balance, and eternal renewal.

THE DARKSIDE

In a peaceful village surrounded by serene hills, two brothers lived whose destinies were intertwined by a powerful bond. The elder brother, Draven, and the younger, Moldark, shared a connection as strong as the roots of the ancient oaks that encircled their abode. The village was known for their deep reverence of the Phoenix Stone, a magical gem that shone with the essence of life. It was said to hold the secrets of power and wisdom, and its guardians were tasked with upholding its eternal radiance. The villagers would gather at the Phoenix Stone's shrine to offer prayers, seeking its blessings for their crops, families, and the prosperity of their land. Draven had been mesmerised by the stories of the stone since childhood as the village elder recounted the tales of legendary warriors and mystics who had harnessed the Phoenix Stone's power to protect their people.

On a special evening, as the sun shone brightly and cast a warm, golden light over the village, Draven and Moldark were present with their parents at the Phoenix Stone shrine. The day was a celebration, marking the anniversary of the village's ancestors' discovery of the Phoenix Stone. The atmosphere was filled with reverence, and the villagers gathered around the glowing gem, praying in harmony. Draven observed the Phoenix Stone with great intensity, mesmerising and unsettling. He could sense a mysterious energy emanating from it, calling to him and whispering secrets that only he could hear. Moldark, noticing his brother's unusual fixation, gently nudged Draven and whispered, "What are you thinking, brother?" Draven replied with an unquenchable fire in his

135

eyes, "I want to understand its power, Moldark. I want to harness it for the greater good." Although Moldark could sense the determination in his brother's voice, he couldn't help feeling a sense of unease. Little did they know that this moment would mark the beginning of a path leading Draven down a dark and treacherous journey. Draven made a decision that would alter the course of his fate. He resolved to embark on a perilous journey to seek power from the Phoenix Stone, hoping to harness it for himself. Without a word to his family, Draven set out under the cover of night, leaving behind the familiar comforts of the village and the serene pastures. He ventured into the dark forests and treacherous mountains surrounding the Phoenix Stone shrine, determined to unlock its secrets. The decision to embark on a perilous journey weighed heavily on Draven's heart as he left his village behind. His obsession with the Phoenix Stone had become an insatiable hunger, driving him to seek the power and immortality he believed it held. With every step he took, he felt the allure of the Phoenix Stone, drawing him closer.

Draven risked his life as he journeyed into the wilds surrounding the Phoenix Stone shrine. The path was dangerous, with twisted trees and dark valleys lurking around every corner. Despite the danger, Draven pushed on, driven by his ambition to gain power from the Phoenix Stone and achieve immortality. The first challenge on his journey emerged within the Whispering Grove, a spooky forest shrouded in perpetual twilight where the trees appeared to be sentient beings. Their branches entwined like fingers, and their leaves whispered secrets only the bravest could understand. As Draven delved deeper into the Whispering Grove, the atmosphere grew increasingly eerie. The air was thick with a sense of foreboding, and the trees seemed to lean in closer, threatening to break his resolve. Their tempting voices beckoned him away from the winding paths that twisted and turned, leading him ever deeper into the heart of the grove. This was not just a physical challenge but a psychological one that preyed on Draven's innermost doubts and desires. The trees whispered seductive promises of power, immortality, and dominion, testing Draven's mental fortitude to its limits. But he remained steadfast, clinging to the winding path and resisting the alluring promises that danced like elusive phantoms on the edges of his consciousness. As he pressed deeper into the grove, the voices grew louder, but he drew strength from his unwavering determination to reach his ultimate goal. Hours felt like eternities as Draven navigated the labyrinthine paths, each step a testament to his resilience and steadfast focus. Finally, as dawn's first light pierced the grove's veil of darkness, Draven emerged unshaken. He had conquered the seductive voices and passed the first ten daunting tests on his quest for power and immortality. The Whispering Grove had tested his mental grit and determination to remain faithful to his purpose.

Having overcome the eerie obstacles of the Whispering Grove, Draven continued his quest for power from the Phoenix Stone and immortality, venturing deeper into the dangerous realm surrounding the mystical gem. His next challenge was the Bridge of Shadows, a treacherous and unsettling crossing that tested his courage and determination differently. The Bridge of Shadows was a bridge to destiny, a rickety and precarious structure suspended high above a chasm of impenetrable darkness. Its timeworn planks creaked ominously beneath each step, and its ropes and supports seemed as though they might give way at any moment. Upon approaching it, Draven felt an aura of foreboding thickening the air, starkly contrasting the ethereal beauty of the surrounding landscape. The chasm below was a void of profound obscurity, its depths hidden from sight. It was said that those who fell into the abyss were forever lost to the darkness, their existence erased as if they had never been. Knowing the stakes were high, Draven was driven by an unquenchable desire to reach the Phoenix Stone and claim its power. The Bridge of Shadows tested his courage with each step, battling against the inner demons of doubt and fear. The bridge swayed and groaned under his weight like a living entity, pushing his resolve to its limits. The abyss beneath seemed to beckon with whispered promises of oblivion, attempting to shake his determination. However, Draven's determination and unwavering willpower proved his greatest ally. He pressed forward, one unsteady step at a time, heart pounding, his eyes fixed on the far end of the bridge where the Phoenix Stone's radiant glow beckoned with an otherworldly allure. Turning back was not an option; his pursuit of power had brought him too far to falter. The journey across the Bridge of Shadows was a test of mettle, requiring physical balance and mental fortitude. Draven's focus remained unbroken, and his willpower prevailed over the creeping shadows that sought to engulf him. He emerged victorious from this harrowing trial, with each step bringing him closer to the other side. He had proven his courage, determination, and unyielding desire to attain the power of the Phoenix Stone. Once a symbol of treacherous uncertainty, the bridge was now a testament to his unshaken resolve. As he stepped onto solid ground, he knew the journey ahead would only become more perilous and the tests more demanding. Draven demonstrated that he possessed the strength of character and the indomitable will to face whatever challenges lay in wait. The Bridge of Shadows was behind him, and the Phoenix Stone's radiant allure beckoned, promising untold power and the possibility of immortality.

Having successfully crossed the Bridge of Shadows, Draven's journey to harness the Phoenix Stone's power and attain immortality led him deeper into the treacherous realm surrounding the mystical gem. The third trial, the Tempest Peaks, was a harrowing test that would challenge his physical strength, unwavering determination, and tenacity. The Tempest Peaks were a range of towering mountains that seemed to pierce the heavens. Their peaks disappeared into the swirling mists above, and the air was thick with an unrelenting tempest. Howling winds lashed at the rocky slopes, threatening to hurl any who dared to traverse them into the abyss below. Draven faced a perilous ascent as he ventured further into this tumultuous terrain. The rocky ledges were slick with rain, and the gales howled with such force that they seemed to have a life of their own. The path before him was a precarious maze of narrow footholds, sharp crags, and treacherous cliffs. With each step, the gusts of wind sought to knock him off balance, as if nature itself conspired to thwart his progress. Yet, Draven clung to the rocky ledges with a tenacity born of sheer determination. His fingers ached, his muscles burned, and his heart raced with the adrenaline of survival. The tempest raged on, unrelenting in its fury, but Draven pressed forward. He knew that to turn back now would mean failure, and his relentless pursuit of power drove him ever upward. The very elements seemed to test his resolve, daring him to continue. The path grew steeper, the winds fiercer, and the rocky terrain more unforgiving as he ascended further into the Tempest Peaks. Each step was a battle against the forces of nature, a testament to his sheer willpower and unwavering commitment to his quest. The mountains sometimes conspired to shake him loose as the peaks had taken on a malevolent sentience. Draven's determination was his anchor, and he clung to it as steadfastly as he clung to the rocks. Eventually, Draven emerged from the Tempest Peaks after what felt like an eternity. He stood at the summit, battered and bruised but victorious. The winds that had threatened to toss him into the abyss now seemed to relent as if nature acknowledged his resilience. The Tempest Peaks had tested not only his physical strength but also his indomitable will. Draven had faced the tempest's fury and emerged unbroken, a testament to his unwavering determination to harness the power of the Phoenix Stone and secure immortality.

Having braved the treacherous Tempest Peaks, Draven continued his quest for power and immortality by delving deep into the heart of the mountains. He soon found himself standing before the Cave of Desolation, a foreboding entrance that seemed to swallow the light. As he ventured inside, a sense of isolation and despair consumed him, and the oppressive atmosphere of the cave weighed heavily on him. The silence was deafening, broken only by the echo of his footsteps, and the twisting labyrinth of the cave's depths seemed to stretch into eternity. Draven was confronted with the darkest recesses of his mind, as his inner demons manifested as grotesque apparitions, taunting him with his deepest fears and insecurities. The path before him was treacherous, and every step was a battle against the despair that threatened to overwhelm him. However, Draven refused to yield to the darkness and confronted his inner demons head-on. Through sheer determination and a refusal to give up, he emerged stronger and more persistent from the Cave of Desolation than ever before. The cave had tested his physical strength and inner fortitude, forcing him to confront his doubts and fears and emerge from the darkness a changed man. Draven had found a newfound clarity and purpose, replacing the cave's aura of despair with a sense of hope and determination.

Draven's relentless journey to attain power from the Phoenix Stone and secure immortality led him ever closer to the shrine that held the coveted gem. As he approached the heart of the mystical realm, he encountered a pivotal test that would challenge not his physical prowess but his wit and wisdom—the enigmatic Guardian and their cryptic riddle.

The Guardian was a figure cloaked in mystery, their form shrouded in ethereal mist. Their eyes gleamed with ancient knowledge, and their presence radiated an aura of otherworldly wisdom. They stood as the guardians of the Phoenix Stone shrine, ensuring that only those worthy could pass through to seek the gem's power. As Draven drew nearer to the Phoenix Stone shrine, the Guardian materialised before him, a mysterious presence that seemed to transcend time and space. The Guardian's voice resonated with a melodic, ageless quality as they presented the riddle determining Draven's fate.

The riddle was as follows:
"I am born of water and fire,
Yet I am neither hot nor cold.
I can be gentle as a breeze,
Or fierce as a tempest untold.
What am I?"

The riddle hung in the air, its words laden with hidden meaning and complexity. Draven's mind raced as he pondered the enigma before him. The answer held the key to his passage to the Phoenix Stone, and failure was not an option. Draven, driven by his unyielding desire for power and immortality, meticulously dissected the riddle. He contemplated the elements of water and fire, juxtaposing gentleness and ferocity. He weighed each word and phrase, searching for the elusive solution. After a profound reflection, Draven summoned his response, his voice unwavering as he answered, "The answer to your riddle is 'steam.' It is born of water and fire, exists between hot and cold, can be as gentle as a breeze, or as fierce as a tempest." The Guardian's eyes glittered with approval, and a faint, knowing smile graced their lips.

Draven's clever and astute response had earned him the Guardian's respect and the right to pass through to the Phoenix Stone shrine. With a graceful gesture, the Guardian stepped aside, allowing Draven to continue his quest. As he moved forward, he could feel the weight of the Guardian's ancient gaze upon him, a reminder that wisdom and wit were as essential to his journey as strength and determination. The encounter with the Guardian and the successful resolution of the riddle marked a pivotal moment in Draven's journey. It emphasised that pursuing power and immortality was not solely a matter of physical prowess but also a test of intellect and wisdom. Draven moved forward with a renewed sense of purpose, knowing that each step brought him closer to the Phoenix Stone and its unimaginable power.

Draven delved into the depths of the Phoenix Stone shrine and faced an extraordinary challenge, the Labyrinth of Illusions. This maze was an intricate fusion of reality and fantasy, which created a perplexing and ever-changing environment. It tested Draven's physical abilities, mental acuity, and perception. The entrance to the Labyrinth of Illusions was an imposing archway adorned with intricate patterns that seemed to dance before his eyes. As Draven stepped through, he was immediately enveloped in a world where reality blurred and perception unravelled. The labyrinth's corridors twisted and turned, leading him in seemingly random directions. The walls shifted and morphed, changing from solid stone to shimmering mirages of water, from lush forests to arid deserts, all in the blink of an eye. Each step he took seemed to transport him to a new and unfamiliar landscape where the laws of physics and reality no longer applied. It was a place where time played tricks, with moments stretching into eternity or passing in the blink of an eye. Amidst this bewildering labyrinth, Draven's instincts and discernment were put to the test. He knew that the path ahead was as treacherous as it was elusive and that a misstep could lead him further into the maze or, worse, into the clutches of his delusions. With each decision, he had to trust his judgment and intuition, as the shifting landscapes and illusions challenged his ability to distinguish reality from fantasy. He was constantly confronted with choices that had the potential to lead him closer to the Phoenix Stone or deeper into the labyrinth's intricate web. At times, he would encounter apparitions that seemed so genuine, phantom figures beckoning him forward or whispering cryptic messages, making it increasingly difficult to discern fact from fiction. Draven's resolve was tested as he navigated the labyrinth's ever-changing corridors, his determination to reach the Phoenix Stone unwavering. As he pressed forward, the maze seemed to sense his resolve, throwing increasingly intricate illusions and challenges in his path. It was a mental and emotional gauntlet, forcing him to confront his doubts and fears, question his perceptions, and rely on his inner strength. Draven experienced moments of frustration, disorientation, and self-doubt in the depths of the Labyrinth of Illusions. But he knew that turning back was not an option, having come too far, and the power of the Phoenix Stone beckoned him like a distant beacon in the shifting darkness. After navigating the labyrinth's bewildering corridors, Draven emerged into the heart of the shrine, having successfully traversed the Labyrinth of Illusions. He was mentally and emotionally exhausted, but his determination remained unbroken. The encounter with the labyrinth had tested his physical endurance, mental resilience, and discernment.

Draven's gruelling quest to harness the power of the Phoenix Stone persisted, leading him through a series of elemental trials within the shrine's inner sanctum. Each chamber presented a unique elemental challenge, testing Draven's ability to harness the forces of nature and adapt to their formidable energies. The first of these tests was the Chamber of Fire, an inferno that seemed to defy all logic. The flames roared and danced around Draven, their blistering heat threatening to consume him. The challenge was to endure the intensity of the fire while finding a balance between resistance and acceptance. Draven's determination burned as fiercely as the flames, as he understood that the fire represented his inner desires and passions. He embraced its energy and used it to strengthen his resolve rather than allowing it to consume him. The second challenge, the Chamber of Ice, starkly contrasted the first. Draven found himself in a frozen wasteland where the bitter cold threatened to freeze him in his tracks. Here, he was tested on his endurance and ability to withstand the icy grip of doubt and fear. Draven's determination became a beacon of warmth against the frigid surroundings as he navigated the frozen landscape. He refused to succumb to the numbing cold and channelled his inner strength to endure. The ice symbolised the barriers he had to overcome on his quest, and he shattered them with his indomitable will. The third challenge, the Chamber of Earth, was a vast cavern filled with towering rock formations and impenetrable darkness. Here, Draven had to navigate through the oppressive weight of the earth itself, symbolising the obstacles and limitations he faced. Draven found that the earth responded to his determination in the heart of the cavern. He carved his path through the rocky terrain, using the strength of the earth to fortify his resolve. The challenge of the earth was a test of his adaptability and resourcefulness, and he emerged from it with newfound clarity and determination. The final challenge was the Chamber of Water, a place of rushing currents and swirling tides. Draven faced the unpredictable and relentless force of water, symbolising the fluidity of his journey and the need to adapt to changing circumstances. As he navigated the tumultuous waters, Draven's determination became his anchor. He allowed the water's flow to guide him, learning to adapt and flow with the ever-changing currents. The water challenge taught him the importance of flexibility and resilience, and he emerged from it with a sense of adaptability that would serve him well in the trials to come. With the successful completion of the elemental challenges, Draven emerged from the heart of the shrine with a newfound sense of mastery over the forces of nature. He had successfully harnessed fire, ice, earth, and water energies, using them to strengthen his resolve and adaptability. The elemental challenges reminded him that his quest for power and immortality was a test of physical strength and a journey of inner growth and transformation.

After a journey filled with dangerous trials and profound self-discovery, Draven stood before the culmination of his relentless pursuit—the Phoenix Stone itself. It was a moment that had driven him through the labyrinth of illusions, the elemental challenges, and the depths of self-reflection. His determination was unwavering as he reached out to touch the glowing gem, the source of unimaginable power and the key to immortality. The Phoenix Stone pulsed with an otherworldly radiance, casting an ethereal glow upon the chamber that housed it. Draven's hand trembled with anticipation as he touched the gem's surface. At that moment, he felt an electrifying surge of energy course through him, a power that transcended anything he had ever imagined. As the energy flowed into him, Draven's senses were overwhelmed. He could feel the Phoenix Stone's essence intertwining with his own, merging with his very being. It was as if the boundaries between himself and the gem had dissolved, and he became one with its immense power. With a flash of brilliance that illuminated the entire chamber, Draven's transformation was complete. He had relentlessly gained the control he had sought, and his desire for immortality had been granted. He could feel the strength of the Phoenix Stone coursing through his veins, invigorating his body and mind with an unprecedented vitality. Draven stood as a being of unparalleled power and potential. He possessed dominion over the forces of nature, harnessed the elements themselves, and could command the very fabric of reality. The Phoenix Stone had granted him the ability to reshape the world to his whim, to bend reality to his desires, and to wield power that could rival even the gods. But as the initial rush of power subsided, Draven was left with a profound sense of responsibility and understanding. Now, with the Phoenix Stone's revelation and the weight of his choices, he had the opportunity to make a difference, use his power for the greater good, and seek a destiny shaped not only by ambition but also by wisdom and compassion.

After gaining the unimaginable power from the Phoenix Stone, Draven's mind became consumed by self-obsession and pride. The strength coursing through him was intoxicating, and he believed himself invincible. However, his judgment became clouded, and he contemplated a dangerous course of action. Draven's initial thoughts centred around destroying the Phoenix Stone, the source of his newfound power. In his twisted logic, he believed that eliminating the gem would ensure no one else could seek the same power, securing his dominance and immortality. His obsession with power had blinded him to the consequences of his actions. Draven had become so enamoured with his might that he could not think straight. He saw the Phoenix Stone not as a source of incredible potential but as a threat to his supremacy, a potential challenge to his newfound reign.

In his effort to shatter the glowing gem that had given him unfathomable strength, a brilliant light burst forth from the Phoenix Stone, so powerful that it felt like it pierced the very fabric of reality. The radiant energy from the Phoenix Stone embraced Draven, lifting him and taking him to a place of dazzling luminosity. He was surrounded by a spectacular, searing light that overwhelmed his senses, leaving him feeling disoriented. The light seemed to have its awareness, and it fought against Draven's attempts to destroy the gem. Since they share the same power, the light couldn't kill Draven. Draven vowed to come back and eradicate the Phoenix Stone.

Driven by his pride and obsession with power, Draven descended further into the abyss of evil. He no longer recognised the person he had once been, who had embarked on a quest filled with trials and self-discovery. Instead, he had become a ruthless and tyrannical figure, a force of darkness whose lust for power knew no bounds. The roots of his descent into evil lay in his overwhelming pride and avarice. Draven's ego had swelled to titanic proportions, leading him to view himself as a deity above reproach. He believed that his power entitled him to make decisions that would shape the world to his liking, regardless of the cost to others. Draven's intentions turned darker, so he acted upon his evil desires. He subjugated those who opposed him and attempted to reshape the world in his image. His actions grew increasingly ruthless and tyrannical as he used his newfound abilities to further his ambitions at any cost.

Draven's pursuit of dominance left destruction and despair in his wake. His actions led to suffering and upheaval as he bent the world to his will with an iron fist. The qualities that had driven him to seek power in the first place—ambition, determination, and an unyielding desire for immortality—had now transformed him into an evil force. Draven's transformation into an antagonist was a cautionary tale of the corrupting influence of power and pride. It was a stark reminder that even the noblest intentions could be twisted when driven to extremes. His descent into evil was a tragic consequence of his unchecked ambition, a stark contrast to the lessons he had learned during his journey through the Phoenix Stone shrine.

COSMIC CONVERGENCE

Aidan and his fellowship found themselves on the brink of a monumental confrontation in this divine theatre of universal forces, where boundaries blurred and dimensions intertwined. The cosmic energies surrounding them crackled with excitement as if the universe held its breath in anticipation of the imminent battle. The Phoenix Stone, a symbol of purity and rebirth, stood at the centre of the conflict, emanating its celestial essence. They arrived at the Phoenix Stone shrine, a place in the Celestial Oasis.

Bathed in the pale, ethereal glow of the Phoenix Stone, a scene of eerie confrontation unfolded. Aidan, the unwavering protagonist, and his companions—Lirael, Kaelen, Nalorin and Ophelia—stood in a solemn semicircle, their gazes fixed upon the figure that loomed before them like an evil spectre. It was Draven. The atmosphere within the chamber was palpable with an unsettling heaviness. This tension hung like an ominous prelude to the impending clash. The chamber walls seemed to pulse with otherworldly energy as if bearing witness to a confrontation transcending the ordinary bounds of reality. Draven stood at the epicentre of this surreal tableau. Cloaked in shadows that clung to him like a sinister shroud, his form was a study in contrasts. His presence exuded an aura of malice, a darkness that seemed to warp the fabric of the space around him.

Draven's transformation into an antagonist had been a descent into cruelty and tyranny. This unsettling metamorphosis had torn the bonds asunder. What looked like a relationship defined by the

147

shared power of Phoenix Stone had evolved into a bitter rivalry fueled by a relentless pursuit of power. Their exchange of words was fraught with an unspoken acknowledgement that their final showdown was inevitable, that the journey that had brought them to this moment had been one of irrevocable change. "Draven," Aidan's voice rang out, steady but laden with a feeling of profound sorrow. "It doesn't have to end like this. The darkness that has consumed you can be dispelled. You can still choose a different path to redemption and healing." Draven's response was a chilling and hollow laughter that cut through the chamber like a bone-chilling wind. It was a laughter devoid of warmth or humanity, a haunting sound that seemed to crawl beneath the skin of all who heard it. It was a stark reminder of the hostility that had taken root in his heart. This malignancy had torn him away from the light. "Redemption? Healing?" Draven sneered, his eyes smouldering with an unnatural fire. "I have no use for such feeble notions. The only path I walk is one of power and domination."

The weight of those words hung in the air like a dark omen, casting a pall over the chamber. Aidan and his companions exchanged sombre glances, knowing Draven's thirst for power had led him down a treacherous and unrelenting path. Aidan grappled with the unsettling realisation that the battle that loomed on the horizon was not only a test of their abilities but also a test of their resolve— a resolve to confront the darkness that had enveloped Draven and bring an end to his reign of evil, no matter the cost.

The chamber of the Phoenix Stone shrine crackled with tension as the confrontation between Aidan, Lirael, Kaelen, Ophelia, and the transformed Draven escalated into a cataclysmic clash of elemental forces. Draven, consumed by malevolence, summoned the elements themselves in a relentless onslaught that threatened to destroy everything in its path.

The battle unfolded with a deafening roar as Draven's mastery over the elements became evident. It was as if the chamber itself had become a battleground for the primordial forces of nature. Flames erupted from his outstretched hands, dancing and swirling in a fiery ballet of destruction. The fire licked at the stone floor, leaving scorching marks in its wake, and the air grew searingly hot.

Aidan, the unwavering protagonist, found himself enveloped by the searing heat. His power, drawn from the Phoenix, allowed him to harness the element of fire. Flames danced in his eyes as he retaliated with a controlled burst of fire, creating a fiery barrier that shielded his companions from Draven's fiery onslaught. Lirael, the extraordinary water mage, rose to the challenge. With a graceful wave of her hand, she summoned torrents of water from the air. These cascading waves swirled and twisted in defiance of gravity, forming a watery shield that intercepted Draven's fiery attacks. Steam hissed and billowed as the fire met water, creating a mesmerising clash of elements. Kaelen, the monk with mastery over windshaper techniques, stood firm amidst the elemental chaos. Her ability over air and wind allowed her to manipulate the atmosphere. With a focused breath, she summoned gusts of wind that swirled around her, creating a protective buffer that deflected the fiery projectiles. The chamber echoed with the sound of howling winds.

Nalorin, the guardian of the earth, rooted himself to the stone floor. His connection to the earth allowed him to command the ground beneath him. He sent tremors through the chamber with a mighty stomp, causing the stone to rise and form a formidable wall of rock and earth. Draven's fire crashed against it, his flames sizzling and dissipating upon impact.

Ophelia, who had been transformed into a Cosmic being through the power of the Phoenix Stone, radiated an otherworldly aura. Her abilities transcended the mere elements, and she reached into the cosmic energies that bound the universe together. She summoned celestial powers that manifested as swirling orbs of energy with a gesture. These orbs acted as a counterforce, absorbing Draven's fiery attacks and converting them into bursts of radiant light.

The chamber itself trembled and groaned under the intensity of the elemental onslaught. It seemed to bear witness to a battle that defied the laws of nature—a battle where fire, water, wind, earth, and cosmic forces clashed in a dazzling display of power and chaos. Draven's malevolent laughter persisted amidst the elemental fury, his relentless assault a testament to the darkness that had consumed him. Flames, torrents of water, howling winds, and shifting earth continued to swirl and collide, creating a mesmerising and terrifying spectacle. The battle raged on, each elemental force vying for dominance. The air seemed charged with an electric energy as the combatants pushed their abilities to the limit. It was a battle that tested their resolve, a battle where they fought not only to defend themselves but also to reach the core of Draven's darkness.

As the elemental onslaught continued, it became evident that Draven's mastery over the elements was formidable. His malevolence had granted him unprecedented control, and he wielded the elemental forces with a chilling precision. It was a stark reminder of their immense challenge—a challenge not only of power but of confronting the darkness that had taken root in Draven's soul. Their greatest weapons were unity, mastery over the elements, and unwavering resolve.

In a moment of profound darkness and desperation, Draven unleashed an evil force that sought to consume Ophelia, the Cosmic being of radiant light. It was a dire moment, as the very essence of Ophelia was threatened by the encroaching darkness. As Draven's darkness closed in on her, it seemed for an instant that Ophelia's light would be extinguished forever. The chamber was imbued with an eerie stillness, a silence that hung heavy in the air. The companions watched in horror as Ophelia's radiant form was eclipsed by the malice that sought to engulf her.

But then, a transformation began to take shape from the depths of the engulfing darkness. Ophelia's form trembled as if wracked by intense internal conflict. Her radiant light, though dimmed, fought valiantly against the encroaching darkness. And then, in a breathtaking burst of radiant energy, Ophelia emerged from the abyss like the mythical Phoenix, rising from the ashes of her own despair. Her form blazed with an intensity that defied description, a luminosity that outshone even the most brilliant stars. The transformation was awe-inspiring, a testament to Ophelia's resilience and the power of the Phoenix Stone that coursed through her. As the darkness was repelled, it seemed to recoil in the face of her radiant rebirth. In that moment, Ophelia had become something greater than herself—a being of cosmic light, a symbol of renewal and transformation. Her presence in the chamber was a beacon of hope, a reminder that even in the darkest times, the light of resilience and inner strength could prevail. Draven, momentarily taken aback by this unexpected transformation, found himself facing an adversary whose power transcended the elemental forces he had harnessed. Ophelia's radiant energy surged forth, pushing back the encroaching darkness and creating a protective barrier around her. The chamber seemed to respond to her transformation, bathed in a dazzling and ethereal radiance that banished the shadows. It was as if the very Phoenix Stone, the source of their power, had recognised Ophelia's unwavering spirit and had granted her the strength to rise above the darkness. As Ophelia, reborn as the Phoenix, spread her wings of light, the companions felt a surge of renewed hope. Draven's malevolence had been thwarted, at least for the moment, and they knew their determination to confront the darkness that had taken root in his soul was stronger than ever. The battle continued, but now Draven faced an adversary transformed by the power of renewal and resilience. Ophelia, the Cosmic Phoenix, stood as a living testament to the indomitable nature of the human spirit and the capacity to rise above even the darkest of circumstances.

As the elemental chaos raged around them, Aidan and his companions knew that a momentous decision had to be made. Draven's malevolence had reached an unprecedented height. They needed to marshal their own elemental powers—fire, ice, earth, and water—to counter the darkness that threatened to consume them and the very essence of the Phoenix Stone itself. Aidan, the unwavering protagonist, stood at the forefront of this elemental convergence. He channelled the fiery power of the Phoenix, flames dancing in his eyes as he summoned the elemental force of fire. The intensity of his determination was matched only by the blazing inferno that radiated from his being. Beside him, Lirael, the extraordinary water mage, was a vision of serene determination. With graceful gestures, she harnessed the fluidity of water, forming shimmering barriers and cascading waves that would protect them from Draven's onslaught of darkness. Her mastery over the element was a testament to her unwavering resolve. Kaelen, the monk with mastery of windshaper techniques, stood as a guardian of the wind. Her connection to air allowed her to manipulate the atmosphere itself. With focused breaths, she summoned gusts of wind that swirled around the companions, forming an ethereal buffer against the encroaching darkness. Her presence was a testament to her unyielding spirit. Nalorin, the guardian of the earth, was a steadfast anchor in the tumultuous battle. His command over the ground beneath them allowed him to shape formidable rock and earth walls. Draven's malevolence crashed against these impervious barriers, his darkness sizzling and dissipating upon impact. Nalorin's strength was unwavering. And then there was Ophelia, transformed into the Cosmic Phoenix, radiant and resplendent. She held within her the power of the Phoenix Stone itself, a force that transcended the mere elements. Her presence was a beacon of hope and renewal, and transformation.

As Aidan and his companions gathered their elemental powers, they felt a profound unity—a convergence of purpose that defied the chaos surrounding them. With synchronised determination, they channelled their energies toward Ophelia, recognising that she could stop Draven's reign of darkness. Ophelia, a being of cosmic light, radiated with an intensity that was blinding to behold. The elemental forces that had threatened to overwhelm them seemed to submit themselves to her, bowing to the radiant power she embodied. It was as if nature itself acknowledged her as a force beyond compare. With a gesture that seemed to encompass the very universe, Ophelia unleashed the combined might of their elemental powers—a dazzling display of light and energy that defied the laws of nature. The chamber itself was illuminated with a brilliance that rivalled the sun, casting aside the oppressive darkness that had taken root. Draven's malevolence was purged by the overwhelming force of their elemental convergence in that profound moment of transformation. He was engulfed by the radiant energy, his form disintegrating into particles of darkness cast into an abyss of their own making.

As the darkness closed around him, Draven found himself in a state of profound isolation and despair. Stripped of the power he had ruthlessly sought, he was left alone with his own thoughts and regrets. The abyss symbolised not only his fall from grace but also the consequences of his actions—the destruction he had wrought, the lives he had disrupted, and the suffering he had caused. It was a moment of reckoning for Draven, a stark realisation of the darkness that had consumed his soul. The power he had sought had been turned against him, casting him into a void of his own making. He was left to confront the consequences of his unbridled ambition and malevolence. As the abyss closed around him, Aidan and his companions knew they had made a painful but necessary choice. Draven's reign of darkness had ended, and the Phoenix Stone's power was once again safeguarded, awaiting those who would seek it with wisdom and compassion.

In the chamber of the Phoenix Stone shrine, the journey had come full circle—from the relentless pursuit of power to the depths of darkness and despair. Now, Aidan and his companions stood together, united by their shared purpose and determination to use their powers for the greater good. They knew that their journey was far from over and that challenges and trials were still ahead. But as they looked upon the spot where Draven had once stood, they also knew that they had made the right choice—to stop the darkness and seek a brighter future where the power of the Phoenix Stone could be used to heal and restore rather than to dominate and destroy.

In the wake of the climactic battle with the notorious antagonist, Draven, the entire cosmos appeared to release a collective exhale of relief. The tumultuous realm, previously ravaged by cosmic strife, gradually began to mend, and the universe's equilibrium was again restored to its rightful place. This was a moment of resolute finality, when every loose end of the tale would be neatly tied up, and Aidan's ultimate fate as the Nura'el would come to a long-awaited fruition. Following the epic battle that had taken place in the Celestial Oasis, a remarkable transformation had taken hold of this ethereal sanctuary. Previously a site marked by both sacrifice and cosmic revelation, it had now undergone a metamorphosis into a realm of serene splendour and heavenly rejuvenation, where tranquillity and balance reigned supreme.

The most striking transformation occurred in the heart of the oasis, where its tranquil waters mirrored the celestial stars above with astonishing clarity. Previously, these waters had been stirred with cosmic energies, reflecting the tumultuous nature of their cosmic battles. Now, they lay still, like liquid mirrors that captured the boundless beauty of the night sky. Once overshadowed by the tempest of darkness, the celestial constellations above sparkled with radiant brilliance, casting their shimmering reflections upon the oasis's surface. It was as if the cosmos itself had granted its approval to the profound cosmic balance that had been restored. The therapeutic effects of their triumph extended far beyond the confines of the oasis. The cosmic energies emanated from their hard-fought victory permeated the world, touching every corner with its healing power. The once wilted and tainted flora now stood tall and vibrant, displaying a newfound vitality that had not been witnessed in ages. The leaves of the ancient trees rustled with renewed vigour, and the blossoms of celestial flowers burst forth in a magnificent explosion of colour and fragrance. It was as if the very life force of the world had been revitalised, rejuvenated by the powerful surge of cosmic energies that had flowed through their battle.

Similarly, the fauna had undergone a profound transformation. Once affected by the encroaching darkness, creatures of the land, sea, and sky now thrived with newfound vitality—birds with plumage as brilliant as the stars soared through the cerulean heavens. Aquatic life, once trapped in shadowy depths, now danced with grace and elegance in the crystal-clear waters. The land teemed with creatures, their presence a testament to the renewed vigour that coursed through the world. Having emerged victorious from their cosmic confrontation, the fellowship of Nura'els took a moment to reflect upon the journey that had led them to this moment. The Celestial Oasis, which had served as a place of sacrifice and cosmic revelation, now symbolised their triumph. Its healing waters mirrored the rejuvenation they had brought to their world and the cosmic balance.

Their bonds, forged in the crucible of cosmic battles, had deepened immeasurably. Their unity, an unwavering force of cosmic magnitude, had been the lynchpin in their victory over Draven. Their roles as Nura'els had expanded beyond mere guardians of the Phoenix Stone; they were now stewards of the cosmic order, responsible for preserving the delicate balance of creation.

As they stood by the revitalised oasis, their reflections revealed that their mission was far from complete. The healing of their world was a testament to the enduring power of unity and cosmic understanding, but their duty extended beyond the boundaries of their world. The cosmos itself awaited their vigilance, and the legacy they carried would forever be intertwined with the grand tapestry of the universe.

The radiant flame of the Phoenix Stone, once a symbol of heavenly power, now burned as a beacon of their commitment to preserving balance. The world had healed, and their legacy as cosmic guardians was forever woven into the very fabric of creation, a legacy they would carry with them as they ventured into the boundless expanse of the cosmos, seeking to ensure that balance and harmony prevailed throughout the universe.

With Ophelia by his side and the fellowship as his cosmic family, Aidan embraced his purpose with unwavering dedication. Though the trials and tribulations ahead would be many, he faced them with the knowledge that his role was intertwined with the fabric of the universe itself, his destiny forever entwined with the cosmic harmony that permeated all of existence.

The unity of the fellowship was their greatest strength, a testament to the enduring power of friendship and shared purpose. Together, they faced cosmic anomalies, dark cosmic entities, and celestial wonders, guided by their unwavering commitment to cosmic order. Their journey became a legacy of hope and destiny that will inspire future generations.

THE ETERNAL FLAME

Over time, the chamber of the Phoenix Stone shrine became a place of reverence and contemplation. Aidan and his companions visited it regularly, seeking solace and guidance. The Phoenix Stone whispered ancient wisdom to those who listened, reminding them of balance, compassion, and the responsible use of power. The world beyond the shrine had changed as well. The darkness that Draven had unleashed had left scars. Still, it also ignited a spirit of resilience and unity among the people. The tales of Aidan and his companions had spread far and wide, inspiring others to stand against the forces of darkness and embrace the power of the Phoenix Stone for the greater good.

The Nura'els had forged a new era of cosmic harmony, where the legacy of Aidan and his loyal companions continued to shape the universe's destiny. At the centre of this new age stood the Phoenix Stone, a radiant beacon of energy that symbolised the delicate balance of the cosmos. Its eternal flame was a testament to the enduring strength of their triumphs and revelations. Aidan and his companions had evolved into legendary figures whose renown extended beyond the boundaries of their world. They were no longer mortals but powerful astral guardians entrusted with a solemn duty to safeguard the Phoenix Stone and preserve the equilibrium of the cosmos.

Their unwavering unity had been the foundation of their success, a testament to the enduring strength of their bonds. Ophelia, the wise mentor who had once been mortal but had transformed into a cosmic being of immense power, remained at the heart of their fellowship, guiding them with her profound wisdom. As cosmic guardians, their responsibilities extended far beyond their home world's scope and into the universe's vast expanse. They were cosmic stewards charged with the sacred task of ensuring that the delicate balance of celestial forces was maintained throughout the cosmos. The lessons they had learned and the trials they had faced had prepared them for a journey that spanned the universe itself.

Their cosmic vigil was not a passive one. They actively sought out anomalies and disturbances in the cosmic order, venturing into the far reaches of the universe to address any threats to the equilibrium. Their journey took them to distant galaxies, enigmatic nebulae, and ancient star systems, where they encountered celestial phenomena that defied mortal comprehension. They grew stronger, wiser, and more attuned to the cosmos with every mission. Their journey was a never-ending one, but they stood ready to face any challenge that came their way in their quest to preserve the cosmic balance.

One of the most significant challenges faced by the cosmic guardians was the existence of celestial rifts, which could cause the fabric of spacetime to tear apart and potentially destroy the universe's balance. These rifts were like cosmic wounds that threatened the very structure of the cosmos, and the fellowship was equipped with their vast cosmic knowledge and the radiant power of the Phoenix Stone to confront them. By channelling the Phoenix Stone's energy, they could mend the cosmic fabric and act as a cosmic glue that held the universe together. Each successfully mended rift was a victory for the forces of cosmic order, a testament to the Nura'els' unwavering commitment to their duty.

However, not all cosmic challenges were physical in nature. The guardians also encountered malevolent dark astral entities that were ancient beings of immense power and whose sole purpose was to disrupt the delicate equilibrium of the universe. These entities thrived on chaos and sought to plunge the cosmos into eternal darkness, which would have catastrophic consequences for all.

In the face of these cosmic adversaries, Aidan and his companions demonstrated not only their physical prowess but also their profound understanding of the cosmic forces at play. They engaged in battles of cosmic ideologies, challenging the evil desires of these entities with their unwavering commitment to preserve cosmic harmony.

As cosmic guardians, they were not mere spectators of the universe's grandeur. They actively preserved cosmic harmony, ensuring that the cosmic symphony continued to play in perfect resonance. Their journey was a celebration of the cosmos, a profound exploration of the universe's mysteries, and a testament to the enduring power of unity, understanding, and the radiant flame of the Phoenix Stone. Their legacy, which was once confined to the boundaries of their world, had become a cosmic legend. Their heroic deeds were celebrated across galaxies, and astral travellers and celestial historians alike told their stories. They were a symbol of hope, a beacon of light in the vast expanse of the universe, and a reminder that the forces of cosmic order would always prevail over the details of chaos.

The Phoenix Stone, with its radiant energy and enduring flame, continued to be the centrepiece of their cosmic journey. It pulsed with the rhythm of the cosmos, its luminous glow a testament to the Nura'els' unwavering commitment to their duty. The Phoenix Stone was not just a source of power but a symbol of cosmic harmony, a beacon of light that guided them through the cosmic expanse. With each use of its energy, they could preserve the universe's balance and ensure that the cosmic symphony played on.

The legacy of the Nura'els is one that has been forged through countless cosmic battles, illuminated by the radiant flame of the Phoenix Stone. It transcends the very boundaries of time and space. It is a legacy that is deeply rooted in the concept of cosmic guardianship, unity, and an unwavering commitment to preserve the delicate balance of the universe. As the cycles of time continue to turn and the ages shift, the legacy of the Nura'els has endured, its impact echoing throughout the vast expanse of the cosmos. Over time, new generations of cosmic guardians have stepped forward to answer the call of destiny. These chosen few are handpicked for their exceptional courage, unwavering strength, and steadfast commitment to upholding the cosmic order. Inspired by the radiant example set by their predecessors, these individuals are driven by the teachings of Aidan, Ophelia, and the esteemed fellowship that has come before them. Through the teachings of these great cosmic guardians, future generations can draw from a wellspring of inspiration and knowledge. The Nura'els' legacy has become a beacon of hope and guidance for those who seek to follow in their footsteps and uphold the cosmic balance for generations to come.

The initiation into the ranks of the Nura'els was a deeply sacred and cosmic ceremony. Recruits from various worlds and galaxies journeyed to a gathering beneath the shimmering stars to pledge allegiance to the cause. The Phoenix Stone, a living embodiment of cosmic harmony, presided over the ceremony, its radiant energy blessing the chosen few. Ophelia, now a revered cosmic mentor, played a pivotal role in the training and guidance of the recruits. Her wisdom, deepened by aeons of existence, illuminated their path and instilled in them the values of selflessness, unity, and a profound understanding of the universe's delicate balance. She was not just a mentor but a living testament to the transformative power of cosmic guardianship. Under Ophelia's tutelage, the new generation of Nura'els delved deeply into the teachings of their predecessors. They studied the cosmic forces that shaped the universe, learned the intricate dance of celestial phenomena, and cultivated their connection to the Phoenix Stone. This connection pulsed with the heartbeat of the cosmos itself.

The radiant energy of the Phoenix Stone continued to touch the lives of countless beings across the universe. It had become more than just a power source; it was a cosmic symbol of hope and renewal. The Phoenix Stone's luminous glow served as a beacon of light in times of darkness, healing those who had lost their way and renewing to a universe in constant flux. Indeed, the Phoenix Stone was a shining example of cosmic harmony's profound and transformative power. The Phoenix Stone's power was awe-inspiring, particularly its ability to mend cosmic rifts. These rifts were tears in the fabric of spacetime, and powerful celestial events or disturbances often caused them. However, the Nura'els were able to harness the Phoenix Stone's energy and use it as a cosmic adhesive to stitch together these torn threads of the universe. The process was a collective effort that required the coordination and collaboration of many guardians, but the result was always worth it.

Each repaired rift served as a powerful symbol of the Nura'els' enduring legacy. These healed wounds were a testament to the forces of light and the ultimate triumph of cosmic order over chaos. Beyond that, they were a tangible reminder of the essential duty that the guardians had as celestial protectors and defenders.

In addition to its healing properties, the Phoenix Stone's radiant energy also played a crucial role in preserving celestial harmony. The stone's cosmic resonance acted as a stabiliser, helping to prevent cataclysmic events and maintain the delicate balance of heavenly forces. This meant that planets, stars, and even entire galaxies benefited from its soothing influence, ensuring that the cosmic symphony continued to play in perfect resonance.

As the Nura'els journeyed through the cosmos, they encountered various celestial phenomena. They witnessed the birth of new stars in stellar nurseries, where the formation of celestial giants was a marvel to behold. They observed the celestial ballet of binary star systems, where two stars circled each other in a cosmic waltz. And they even saw the majesty of galactic collisions, where the gravitational forces of vast astral entities reshaped the destiny of entire galaxies. For the guardians, each of these cosmic events was a powerful reminder of the intricate interplay of celestial forces that governed the universe. It was a reminder that their duty as heavenly protectors extended far beyond simply defending against cosmic threats. Instead, they were responsible for ensuring that the delicate balance of cosmic forces was maintained at all times, in even the smallest of ways.

Their journey was a testament to the enduring power of unity, understanding, and the radiant flame of the Phoenix Stone. They stood ready to face the challenges of the universe with unwavering resolve, leaving behind a legacy of cosmic harmony, unity, and the enduring flame of the Phoenix Stone that would forever illuminate the cosmos. Their story was a shining thread in the grand tapestry of the cosmos, a reminder that the light of unity and understanding would always prevail. The legacy of the Nura'els continued to grow, celebrated across worlds and galaxies, inspiring recruits chosen for their commitment to the cosmic order.

The Phoenix Stone's radiant energy touched countless beings across the cosmos, symbolising hope and the enduring power of selflessness and unity. Even in the darkest times, its light never faded, offering healing and renewal to the universe.

Aidan and his companions' journey transcended time and space, fulfilling their destiny as Nura'els. As they embarked on their eternal journey, they remained steadfast in their resolve to face the challenges of the cosmos, leaving behind a legacy of cosmic harmony and the enduring flame of the Phoenix Stone.

ABOUT THE AUTHOR

Mastan Momin is a passionate writer who embarked on their literary journey purely out of love for storytelling. Writing started as a hobby, a way to escape into different worlds and explore the depths of imagination. What began as a personal pastime soon evolved into something much more profound. "The Guardians of the Phoenix Stone" is Mastan's debut work, a labour of love that encapsulates his dedication to storytelling. While he may have started as an author by chance, his passion and commitment have propelled him to share his imagination with a wider audience.

Printed in Great Britain
by Amazon